Teacup Pigs, Micro Pigs, Miniature Pigs

The Complete Owner's Guide

The must have guide for anyone passionate about owning, breeding, or raising Teacup Pigs, Micro Pigs, Miniature Pigs or Mini Pigs

by

Elliott Lang

Published by IMB Publishing

© 2011 IMB Publishing

Printed and bound in Great Britain by Lightning Source.

ISBN : 978-0-9566269-2-9

A catalogue record of this book is available at the British Library.

The love of a pig is as wonderful and warm as the love that you experience in your family. I am truly blessed to have a wonderful family who have introduced me into the world of micro pigs.

I would like to thank my wonderful children who have inspired me to create a complete guide on this wonderful pet and to my wife who has been a constant support as I have finished this labour of love.

This book is for them and for all the micro pigs and micro pig lovers throughout the world.

Table of Contents

Chapter One: Introduction

Micro pigs. Not much else needs to be said to bring a smile to someone's face. There is little doubt that a pig can be cute, especially when they come in a smaller size and it is their looks and their personality that is making them a very popular pet to own.

One question that I am constantly being asked is are they simply a fad and do they make great pets?

First, micro pigs are no more a fad than any other animal that is kept as a pet. We see crazes come and go and many times, a popular movie or television show will cause thousands of people to rush out and purchase animals such as specific dog breeds like a

Dalmatian. They see some cute puppy perform wondrous tasks on the television and suddenly that breed is a popular breed.

If you are to look closely, that is a craze and it results in thousands of unwanted dogs in

shelters every year. While you could say that a micro pig is a fad for some, the simple question to ask is "How many pigs do you find in those shelters?" I have found over the years that many micro pig owners take time in selecting their pig. They have to wait for litters and usually these waiting lists are long and people who were buying for a craze are often weeded out before they can even purchase a micro pig.

Second, micro pigs make excellent pets. They are intelligent enough to train and they can bond very well with their owners. However, it is important to realize that micro pigs are not small. Okay, there, I said it from the very beginning and I want to stress this. Micro pigs are not small. Sure, they are smaller than an average sized pig, and they are even smaller than a small pig, but a full grown micro pig will average around the same size as a medium sized dog.

They will not remain in a teacup for their entire life and you should be prepared for your pig to get bigger.

But despite their size, micro pigs are popular because they are an alternative to the average pet. They have a unique temperament that is charming and calm and is as layered, or even more layered, than any other pet temperament that you bring into your home.

This is a versatile and wonderful animal and while they have caught a bad break being considered a fad, it doesn't detract from the overall effect these little pigs have on both a home and a heart.

In fact, micro pigs can make extremely good pets. Their small size allows them to live anywhere that a medium sized dog could live and their intelligence has them as easily trained as even the smartest dog breeds. They are usually very healthy animals and while it may not seem like the case, they are a clean animal.

Of course, all of these things I will go over later in this book but for now, let's just agree that the world of micro pigs is an interesting and versatile world filled with the sweetest of creatures.

This book is designed to take you to that world and introduce you to everything you need to know about micro pigs. Whether you are new to micro pig ownership or have years of experience, everything you need to know about the care and raising of a micro pig can be found in this book.

This book takes you through breeding and caring for both a pregnant sow and her young piglets after they are born. So whether you are looking to branch out into the world of micro pig breeding or not, you have definitely opened the right book to tell you everything you need to know about owning a micro pig.

So while the name of the pig may be small in stature and may bear a word for small in its name, there is nothing small about the personality of this animal or the love that micro pig owners feel for their cherished pigs. For this reason, there was no doubt to try to create a book that was big enough to cover the world and devotion of micro pigs.

Chapter Two: About a Pig

It all starts with a pig; at least, that is what anyone who owns a micro pig will tell you. There is something wonderful about the animal that is very difficult to put your finger on. You could say that it is their sweet little appearance or their little snorts, or it could be their personality, whatever it is, people who own a micro pig are hooked as far as pets are concerned.

But while we know how wonderful these animals can be, or will know by the end of this book, there are a few questions that everyone has about micro pigs and where they started. This chapter will cover the history surrounding the micro pig as well as the general facts that every potential micro pig owner should know.

History of a Micro Pig

So it all had to start somewhere, but the main problem with micro pigs is that there are many different reasons and places where they come from. If you think about pigs in general, there have always been smaller pigs alongside their larger counterpart. In fact, the first micro or miniature pig can be traced back to the 1980's.

If you are looking for a definitive answer and history of the micro pig, then you aren't going to get it. Micro pigs, like many pet species, have a history that is filled with unknowns and controversy. Sure there are some people that helped the micro pig along but it is difficult to call them the creators of the species.

It is important to note that there are several species of pigs that are known to be smaller and while they are sold as miniature pigs species, they are not considered to be "the" micro pig. In fact, many experts agree that the micro pig as we know it today was developed from the Gloucester Old Spot pig breed.

But smaller pigs have always been around and during the 1980's, scientists realized the benefit of research involving pigs. They also realized that a full sized pig posed a number of problems for research facilities so they began using smaller pigs. During this time, one of the suppliers for research pigs began to breed down his stock. This resulted in the creation of the mini pig. While this is often touted as the basis for the micro pig, it is important to note that mini pigs were bred solely for research.

But the breeding down of research pigs started something and more and more breeders realized the potential of creating a smaller pig with the personality that people look for in their pets. A number of different pig breeds were bred down and this resulted in a large range of sizes when it comes to the micro pigs. In fact, many organizations, including Defra (Department for Environment, Food and Rural Affairs) in the UK, have defined micro pigs as any breed of pig that has been bred down through many generations.

The micro pig as we know it today was developed in Cumbria, U.K. and was created by breeding down a number of different breeds including the Potbellied Pig. The efforts of the breeder took about 15 years to produce a pig that had the desired size and personality. In addition to these pigs, a breeder by the name of Chris Murray from Devon, England, spent 9 years breeding down his own pigs, originally known as the Pennywell miniatures.

These pigs became known as the Teacup Pigs, although they are still very much a micro pig, and while the piglets have been featured in teacups, the name was chosen simply because the pigs shared a love of tea with their developer.

So in general, micro pigs have been around for decades, and it has been the efforts of many breeders that have resulted in the creation of the micro pig as we know it today.

General Facts about Micro Pigs

Now that you have been introduced to the history of the micro pig, it is time to really start looking at the different facts surrounding them. Yes, they do have a colorful personality but in the grand scheme of things, you should know more about your pet before

you invest the money and the time into it. After all, if the micro pig is not a pet for you, then it is better to know it from the start and not after you bring that pig home.

While I will go over many of the topics more thoroughly throughout this book, let's start by answering some of the more frequently asked questions of new and potential micro pig owners.

What is a micro pig?

A micro pig is a small sized pig that is the result of generations of selective breeding to produce a smaller pig.

What is the difference between a micro pig, mini pig and a teacup pig?

Despite some reports that they are different, the micro pig, mini pig and teacup pig are all the same and are actually just different words to describe them. There is no size difference between a micro and teacup pig and the only main difference is that the majority of mini pigs are used for research and are not usually found as pets.

Are micro pigs clean?

Despite the common belief that pigs are dirty, owners of micro pigs are happy to report that their pets are very clean. They prefer to have an area for toileting and an area for sleeping and if they are properly trained, a micro pig will avoid going to the bathroom in the home; which is their sleeping area, and will only go outside in the area that is set up. Remember that housetraining with any pet rests solely on the shoulders of the owner and the training they do with their pig. For more information on housetraining your micro pig, read chapter eight.

Are they okay with children?

Pigs are usually amazing with children; however, they do need to interact with them for this to occur. It is important to remember that micro pigs have been known to be aggressive if they are not properly trained and raised.

Do they do well with other pets?

Micro pigs are amazing with other animals and pets and do very well in a multi pet home. In fact, micro pigs are very social animals and will thrive if there are other animals, specifically another pig in the home. For this reason, many people prefer to have more than one micro pig in their home.

What is the lifespan of a micro pig?

A micro pig generally lives between 15 to 18 years and are known to be fairly healthy animals. This, in turn, often leads to fewer vet bills for your pet until their later years. It is important to note that proper care is important for the longevity of your micro pig.

What colors are micro pigs?

Colors are pretty standard pig colors including the cute pink pig that was made popular with movies such as "Babe", however, the most common colors are black or black and white. They also can be found in pink, pink with black spots, ginger, ginger with black spots or white with black spots.

How long do they take to mature?

Micro pigs mature at different rates but in general, a micro pig will reach maturity at about 2 years of age.

Although size is an important question regarding general facts about micro pigs, since there have been several misconceptions about their size, I will be discussing size later in this book.

Temperament of a Micro Pig

When it comes to temperament, one cannot ask for a more pleasing companion than a micro pig. Generally, these animals are very intelligent and tend to have a docile nature that makes them ideal for any type of family.

They are usually very social animals and they thrive when they are with their owners or with other animals. In fact, a micro pig that is left for too long on their own can become quite destructive so it is important to have a safe, outdoor area for your micro pig when you are away.

Micro pigs usually do very well with other animals since they are social but they can be aggressive, especially if they are not properly trained and have not been spayed or neutered. They do much better in a home with another micro pig to keep them company; however, this is not always necessary and as long as you are providing for their social needs, a single pig in the home is fine.

When it comes to children, the micro pig is usually wonderful. They are generally docile enough not to become aggressive towards children and since many micro pigs can be playful, they can provide children with a playful companion.

One thing that can't be stressed enough is spaying or neutering your micro pig. A pig that has not been altered can go into heat several times a year, sometimes as much as every three weeks. When a female is in heat, she can become aggressive and very hard to manage. She will also make constant squealing noises and all the charm of your piglet will quickly fade. Males are equally as difficult to manage once they reach sexual maturity and they will try to mount just about anything they can find. If you are not breeding pigs, it is imperative that you have your pig altered.

Another important topic to stress is that training is integral to having a well rounded and sweet tempered pig. These are intelligent animals and can learn a number of tricks and behaviours that will make owning a micro pig that much more enjoyable. You should be aware that micro pigs are as big of a responsibility as owning a dog and training should be done during those first few months after you bring you pig home.

Generally, micro pigs will fit into any home, as long as they have ample access to the outdoors. They are usually quiet animals, although they will squeal when they are scared or when they are picked up. While they love being sociable, this is not usually an animal that enjoys being picked up and carried around. They are happiest when they have all four feet on the ground, although they will follow you wherever you go.

Snapshot of a Micro Pig

Common Names: Micro Pig, Mini Pig, Teacup Pig

Average Height: 12 to 20 inches
(30.5 to 50.8 centimeters)

Average Weight: 40 to 65 pounds
(18.2 to 29.5 kilograms)

Common Colours:
Pink
Pink with black spots
Ginger
Ginger with black spots
White with black spots

Lifespan: 15 to 18 years

Health: Very healthy

Size and Your Adult Micro Pig

When it comes to the size of your micro pig, it can be a bit confusing and misleading. In fact, there is no other trait of the micro pig that is more misleading than that of size. Many unethical breeders of micro pigs, along with the media, have cultivated the image of a pig no bigger than a teacup, hence their names.

It is important to remember that the majority of photos seen on the web and in the news are those of piglets. An adult micro pig does not stay that size and they do not remain small for very long. Pigs grow quickly and many can reach full size before they are even a year of age.

Generally, the size of a micro pig is very confusing since many do not have a large amount of height but they do have a fair amount of width to them. They often weigh much more than you would expect and while a micro pig may only reach 20 inches in height, their width makes them closer to a medium or large sized dog.

In addition to this, there really is no guarantee of how large your micro pig will grow. A runt, which is the smallest piglet in the litter, can actually become quite large while the largest piglet in the farrow, or litter, can become the smallest. A good rule of thumb is to look at the parents, and if possible the grandparents, of the piglets to determine the size your pig has the potential to reach; generally, the smaller the parents, the smaller the pig, although this is not always the case.

When you are deciding on a piglet, it is important to remember that this pig will grow to the size of a medium sized dog at the smallest and you should take this into consideration in regards to your home. If your house isn't large enough for a medium sized dog, then it probably isn't large enough for a medium sized pig.

As I have mentioned in the snapshot of a micro pig, the average size is between 12 to 20 inches (30.5 to 50.8centimetres) and 40 to 65 pounds (18.2 to 29.5kilograms). However, one problem is that the size is based on a standard micro pig that has been bred down from Gloucester Old Spot pig breed. Unfortunately, not all pigs that are sold as micro pigs come from this breed and because of this; you can have a significant variation in the size of your micro pig.

Many breeders have begun to cross other breeds of pigs into the micro pig lines and this has led to a significant variation in sizes. Finally, there have been a few breeders that have introduced boars, wild pigs, into the lines to produce a different head shape and color variety and again, this can affect the size of your pig. Some of the more common micro pigs are:

- *Potbelly Pig:* While this is not a micro pig, I have come across the potbelly pig being sold as a micro pig several times. These were originally a very popular breed of pig for pet pigs; however, their size has made them fall out of popularity. A potbelly pig is usually between 16 to 26 inches (40.6 to 66 centimetres) in height and 120 to 200 pounds (54.5 to 90.9kilograms) in weight.
- *Mini Potbelly Pig:* Slightly smaller than a regular potbelly pig, the mini potbelly still has a fair amount of size and weight to them. Generally, they are 15 to 16 inches (38.1 to 40.6 centimetres) in height and can weigh 80 to 120 pounds (36.4 to 54.5 kilograms).
- *Micro Potbelly Pig:* These are considered to be the smallest potbelly pig that you can purchase and they are similar to the micro pig that many people purchase. In fact, some micro potbelly pigs are sold as micro pigs even though they can have a significant amount of weight to them. On average, the micro potbelly pig is between 12 to 14 inches (30.5 to 35.6 centimetres) and weigh between 60 to 80 pounds (27.3 to 36.4 kilograms).
- *Micro Pig:* Also known as teacup pigs, these are the pigs that have been bred down from the Gloucester Old Spot. The average micro pig is between 12 to 20 inches (30.5 to 50.8

centimetres) in height and 40 to 65 pounds (18.2 to 29.5 kilograms) in weight.

- *African Pygmy Pig:* A miniature pig that has a straight back as opposed to the slough back of the potbelly pig, the African Pygmy Pig is not as commonly seen as other micro pigs. On average, they tend to be slimmer in build and while they can reach the average height of 14 to 22 inches (35.6 to 55.9 centimetres), their weight usually averages out at 20 to 40 pounds (9.1 to 18.2 kilograms).

- *Ossabaw Island Pig:* These pigs have the height of a micro pig, but they are usually a bit larger and heavier than an average micro pig. The average weight of an Ossabaw Island Pig is between 25 to 90 pounds (11.4 to 40.9 kilograms), although their average height is between 14 to 20 inches (35.6 to 50.8 centimetres).

- *Yucatan Pig:* Buyers should be cautious if they are purchasing a Yucatan pig, also known as a Mexican Hairless Pig, since these pigs can range in size significantly. Most are between 16 to 24 inches (40.6 to 61 centimetres) in height; however, they can grow up to 200 pounds (90.9 kilograms) if you do not purchase a smaller variation. It is important to note that even a small sized Yucatan pig can grow to between 50 to 100 pounds (22.7 to 45.5 kilograms).

- *Juliani Pig:* These pigs are truly the micro pig that many people are looking for, but again, they can have a significant amount of weight to them. Generally, the Juliani pig averages 10 to 15 inches (25.4 to 38.1 centimetres) in height and 15 to 50 pounds (6.8 to 22.7 kilograms) in weight.

Size Comparison of the Micro Pig

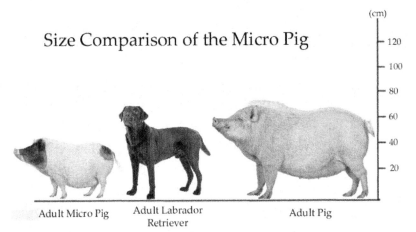

(cm)
120
100
80
60
40
20

Adult Micro Pig   Adult Labrador Retriever   Adult Pig

One thing that I should stress is that every type of pig has a different personality and disposition. Juliani, potbelly, and micro pigs tend to have a gentle disposition, with the Juliani being the more playful of the three. The Ossabaw tend to be very intelligent and have a longer lifespan, with many reaching the age of 25. Finally, the African Pygmy Pig is usually very active and isn't as docile as the other breeds.

As you can see, it is very important to research the size of the pigs before you commit to a micro pig breeder and litter. If the parents are larger than you would like in an adult pig, find a different breeder. Remember that the sweet little piglet is going to grow up and won't remain that size for very long.

Chapter Three: Is a Micro Pig for You?

When it comes to owning any pet, knowing that it is the right one before you purchase is an important part of making the decision. This is important whether you are buying a fish, a dog, or a bird and it is just as important when you are buying a more unusual pet such as a pig.

Remember that you should never purchase a pet simply because it is a fad. You should make sure that you have solid reasons for wanting the pet and that those reasons will see you through the next 18 years with your pet. Unlike some species of pets, micro pigs can have a very long lifespan and when you commit to a piglet, you could be committing to a quarter of a century of care at the latest.

If that thought has made you pause, then you should reassess whether or not you want to bring home a micro pig or at the very least, take your time before finalizing your decision. The last thing that anyone would want is for a pig to have to be rehomed.

But it isn't all about emotional wants and knowing that it is an ideal pet for you. You also have to think about your home, the type of setting you live in and also the size of your home. Trust me, I have a list of animals I would love to own but my house is just not large enough for them.

Some considerations that you should take on deciding if a micro pig is right for you are:

Do you rent or own?

This might not seem like a huge problem if you rent since owning a pet is not something that only a home owner can enjoy but micro pigs need a specific amount of living space and if you rent, you may not always be able to provide the type of living space that your pig needs. Think about the long term before deciding on a pig so that you are sure you won't have to give up your pig simply because your living arrangement changes.

Do you live in an urban setting or a rural setting?

There is no doubt that micro pigs do much better in a rural setting and it is also much easier to get the proper permits for them if you live in the country, however, because of their size, you can own them in an urban setting. Regardless of where you live, a micro pig does need access to the outdoors so if you have a house in the city, with a small yard, then you have a great spot for your pig.

Do you live in an apartment?

Apartments are not recommended for micro pigs since these animals need to be outside during part of each day. In fact, a pig that doesn't receive enough outdoor time can become destructive and while walks can alleviate some of that, micro pigs thrive when they can go outside and simply root around in a garden.

Can you be a strong owner?

Micro pigs can be aggressive and while they may seem like pushovers, they do need a strong owner who will follow through on rules and training. If they don't have that, they can become the "boss pig" of the house and will take it over. If you find that you are more of a pushover when it comes to animals, then you may want to consider a different pet.

Do you work long hours?

Known to be very social animals, micro pigs can become very destructive and bored if they are left on their own for too long. They do need an owner who will interact with them on a regular basis and isn't gone from the house for extensive periods of time. If your work and commute take you past the ten hour mark for being away from home, you may want to consider a different pet.

Are you looking for an active pet?

And finally, while some micro pigs can be very active, most are docile and can be lazy. If you are looking for a jogging companion, then these may not be the best choice of pet.

As you can see, there are a lot of things to consider regarding micro pigs and whether they will fit into your life, but if you find that you have answered favourably to most or all of the questions in regards to owning a micro pig, then they just might be the perfect pet for you.

Pros and Cons of Micro Pigs

Although I can sing the praises of micro pigs, it is very important to look at the pros and cons of them in an objective way. After all, it does no one any good if I simply list the positives of having such a friendly companion since it won't give you an accurate descripiton of what a micro pig is like.

It is important to, along with answering the questions above, to consider all of the pros and cons of owning a micro pig before you bring one home.

Pros of Micro Pigs

- *They are clean:* Most micro pigs are very clean and they don't usually have a bad smell to them. They prefer to keep their sleeping areas free of feces and they will only go to the bathroom in the designated area they have been trained to go in.

- *They can be litter trained:* Speaking of going to the washroom, micro pigs can be trained to a litter box or trained to go outside.

- *They are social:* Micro pigs are very social animals and they usually bond very quickly with their owners and other members of their family. They thrive when they can interact with their family and are happiest being with them. They are usually very affectionate with their owners.

- ***Micro pigs are very intelligent:*** Known for their intelligence, micro pigs are often compared to an average dog when they are rated for their trainability. They can master a number of different tricks and often approach training in an enthusiastic way.

- ***They are non shedding:*** Micro pigs do not have fur and they do not shed, which makes keeping your house and your clothes free of hair much easier than if you had a dog or a cat.

- ***They are hypo allergenic:*** While I detest saying that animals are completely hypo allergenic, a micro pig comes as close to this as is possible. They do not have fur and their skin composition is very similar to that of humans, which makes them much better for allergy sufferers.

- ***They do well with other pets:*** Another plus for micro pigs is that they can do well in homes with multiple pets. While they thrive with other pigs, they can also do very well mingling with cats and dogs.

- ***They are exceptional with children:*** Since micro pigs are very social animals, they do very well with children and can be an affectionate and playful companion to them.

- ***They are healthy:*** When you choose a micro pig from a reputable breeder who only breeds healthy stock, you have a better chance of having a very healthy pet.

- ***They are a unique pet:*** Finally, micro pigs are a unique pet that very few people have, which can be both a pro and a con.

There are a number of other pros to owning a micro pig, but I find that most of them are personal pros that reflect the nature and living situation of each individual micro pig owner.

Cons of Micro Pigs

- *They can be aggressive:* Micro pigs can be very aggressive if they are not properly trained and handled. They need a strong owner who will be the "boss pig" in the home and if there isn't one there, they can become quite unmanageable.

- *They need outdoor space:* Despite being viewed as a house pet, micro pigs do much better if they are kept outdoors the majority of the time. They can do well in homes but they do need to spend part of their day outside so they will need to have enough outdoor space to really enjoy it.

- *They like to chew:* Pigs have a voracious appetite and micro pigs are no different. They will chew just about anything and they love having things in their mouth. It can be difficult to pig proof your home and you need to be constantly vigilant about keeping things out of reach of your pig, regardless of your pig's age.

- *They are unique:* As I mentioned in the pros, micro pigs are still very unique pets that aren't seen by many and while this can be a wonderful pro, it can also make ownership harder. Generally, hunting down a vet for your pig can be a challenge, especially in an urban setting, and you will need to find a vet that specializes in farm livestock, which can mean higher vet bills. Vacations may be harder for you since many kennels that normally take dogs and other pets are not equipped or knowledgeable about pet pigs and may not be able to accommodate your needs.

- ***They can be difficult to keep:*** If you are buying a micro pig because you are looking for an easy pet, then you should choose a different one. While they can learn quickly and they don't require as much grooming as other pets, they do need a fair amount of maintenance and husbandry. They need to have a constant supply of fresh bedding and they will need ample outside time. They can be quite clingy to their owners and do need daily attention.

- ***They need special licensing:*** The licenses differ depending on the area that you live but in general, micro pigs are still considered to be farm animals, regardless of their size. For this reason, there are certain laws that prohibit farm animals in cities completely and even in town or cities that allow them, special licensing has to be done. You may need special permits to move your micro pig from the breeder's to your home so this can be quite a challenge when you are bringing home your micro pig. I will be looking at licenses in Chapter Five: Bringing Your Micro Pig Home.

- ***They can be overly amorous:*** To put it lightly, an unaltered pig can be very amorous and males will try to mount everything from furniture to people. Females can go into heat every few weeks and can become very difficult to handle during those times.

And there are some key pros and cons to consider before you decide on whether a micro pig is right for you or not.

Chapter Four: Choosing a Micro Pig

Well, you are finally there and you have made the decision that yes, the micro pig is the pet for you. Congratulations on your choice and I am sure that once you bring your micro pig home, you will be overjoyed with the wonderful pet that is sharing your home and your life.

Of course, before you can celebrate your new pet and family member, you need to find the right pig for your home and for you. It can be as simple as going to a breeder and seeing the right pig at the right time, however, many times, it takes a lot more effort than simply looking in classified ads.

In fact, since they are an exotic pet, there are fewer breeders of micro pigs than other animals. Many breeders that have cropped up often advertise larger sized pigs as micro pigs and the unfortunate results are not seen until you have a 200 pound (90.9 kilogram) pig in your home.

Waiting lists are often very common and you could find yourself waiting up to a year before you can bring your pig home. So as you can see, it can be quite a task to find a micro pig that is healthy, affordable and will remain as small as they should be. In this chapter, I will take you through what to look for in a breeder as well as what to look for when you choose the perfect pig for your family.

Finding a Breeder

When it comes to choosing the right breeder for your micro pig, the best piece of advice I can give you is to go with your gut instinct. If you feel like the breeder is not ethical or you get a bad feeling from him or her, go with a different breeder, even if it means waiting a little longer to get the pig of your dreams. It is better to play it safe than to simply purchase from the first breeder you meet.

But there is more to choosing a breeder than simply going with your gut instinct and the very first thing that you will want to do is find one.

First, it can be difficult to find a micro pig breeder since there are not many breeders around. Yes, you can find them from time to time in classified ads and online classified sites, but in regards to finding quality, you often have to look a bit further and deeper than simply clicking online.

But where do you find breeders?

The answer really depends on where you are living. In the United States and Canada, there are actually only a few breeders that offer authentic micro pigs, meaning there are several breeders claiming to produce micro pigs but not actually doing so. In Great Britain, more breeders are available, but again, there are several that are breeding in unethical manners and this has produced some problems in the animals.

Always start by going to local livestock associations since they may have a list of breeders who are breeding pet pigs. There are often a number of different associations that have names and links for breeders of that specific pig. Micro pigs tend to have missing information in regards to this; however, if you are choosing an Ossabaw Island Pig along with several other breeds, then there are some associations for this.

Another great way to find and meet pig and micro pig breeders is to attend local livestock and pig shows. You may not find a micro pig there, but you are sure to hunt down people who can direct you to the right person.

One word of warning about pig shows is that many have auctions. If you do find a micro pig at a pig auction, do not purchase the pig there, no matter how low the bidding starts at. The main reason for this is simply because the average person wouldn't know if a pig is healthy and while it may seem sound at the auction, when you finally get it home, you will quickly realize that it wasn't. There is no way for you to see what type of conditions the pig came from and there are too many unknowns, which can lead to lifelong problems for your pig.

If you do go the route of finding a breeder through a classified, it is very important that you look for certain traits in your breeder. These traits are:

- *Knowledgeable:* Does the breeder know a lot about micro pigs and is he willing to share that information with you. If he seems to be unsure about some things about micro pigs, then it is probably best to find a different breeder.

- *Picky:* If you phone a breeder and they are willing to hand over a pig minutes before you can even say your name, let alone explain your situation, then you really don't want a pig from that breeder. Since these are exotic pets, micro pig breeders tend to be picky about where their pigs are going in an effort to stave off any problems later in the pig's life. If you aren't asked a dozen questions before you even get a maybe, then you should start looking elsewhere.

- *Social:* Okay, this may not be the case with all of them, but any breeder that produce high quality micro pigs will invite people to come and visit their breeding program. If a breeder seems hesitant about letting you come over to see them, then you should probably avoid the breeder since they may be hiding something.

In addition to these traits, it is important to really research your breeder. Find out if they have any references from past breeders and also make sure that their pigs have been checked by a vet for health issues. If they are not getting routine health checks done on their pigs, then there may be some problems that could put your piglet at risk.

You should always tour the facility before you commit to a piglet. One, it should be clean and tidy. If the pigs are kept in small cages or they are kept in a filthy condition, then it is important to leave right away. Two, make sure the pigs look healthy. If they don't, find a different breeder. Three, if the pigs seem large to you, then it would be better to choose a different breeder and litter since you can be almost guaranteed that the piglets of those pigs are going to grow up just as large.

While you are checking on the size of the adult pigs, also check on the overall temperament that you are seeing. Remember that micro pigs are supposed to be social and fairly docile creatures so the parents of the piglets should be as well.

As you are going over the condition of the breeding facilities and looking at the breeding stock, make sure that the breeder has all their paperwork in order. Are the pigs properly vaccinated? Does she have the proper license and permits to own and operate a pig farm? Can she trace her pigs back to the micro pigs that came from Cumbria?

Also make sure that she has all the proper paperwork that is needed for owning and breeding pigs and that she will not allow the piglets to leave until you have yours. Lastly, breeder that will release the piglets to you before they are 8 weeks of old is a breeder to stay clear of. It is imperative for the development of your piglet that he never leaves before he is 8 weeks of age.

If she has all of these things, then move ahead with choosing the right pig for you, however, if she doesn't, then it is better to look for a different breeder. Remember that in the end, if anything you see makes you pause and wonder if the breeder is the right one, then you should decide to look elsewhere for your micro pig.

Choosing the Right Pig

Once you find the right breeder, it is time to choose the right piglet for you. Again, I always stress that you look at the parents of the litter before you look at the actual piglets. Ask yourself if the pigs have a look that you like and also if they are the size you want. Make sure that the pigs were full size when they were bred. The simple way to do this is to ask the pig's age. If they are under 2, there will probably still be some growth and many times, pigs fewer than three can still shoot up a bit.

If they are younger, you can still purchase from that litter but be aware that the pigs may get a bit larger than you had expected. Generally, always get a good look at the breeding facility that you go to visit before you pick out your pet micro pig, please read Finding a Breeder if you haven't already.

When you have checked off everything you need concerning the parents, start looking at the piglets themselves. There are several different colours that you can choose from and if you are choosing a different breed of miniature pig, then you will also have different temperaments.

In regards to colour, there are a number of factors that you should consider. While pink and white are traditional colours that bring to mind Babe, they are not always the best choice. They can be a bit more work since lighter coloured pigs tend to suffer from sunburn more than other pigs. Because of this, there may be a bit more work involved in caring for your little micro pig.

With size, it can be difficult to determine how large or small a micro pig will be and even the most seasoned breeder will be hard pressed to determine. Generally, a good rule of thumb is to look for a smaller piglet if you are looking for a smaller pig but bear in mind that this is not always the case.

Lastly, check to see how social the piglets are. Are they used to be handled, do they like being handled? Remember that pigs love to have all four feet on the ground so even if they squeal when you pick them up; it shouldn't be a pig catching game to touch one. Look for a pig that doesn't seem shy or skittish when you are choosing your pig.

As with all pets, you will need to give some consideration to whether you want a male or female, unless you are taking the recommendations of the breeder. Males are usually more aggressive and try to control the house as the boss pig. It is better for males to be neutered if you are keeping them solely as a pet, especially since males tend to mount anything they can find.

Females are usually more docile and have a sweeter temperament. Again, it is better if they are spayed;

however, even an intact female can be quite docile and usually makes a better companion than an unaltered male. Size wise, there is not much of a difference between the two.

Once you have chosen your piglet, it is very important to take the time to do a health check on the pig. This should be done when you are first selecting your piglet and also when you go back to pick it up. Check the following things on your piglet and also on all the pigs in the litter:

- *Alert and Active:* Healthy pigs, regardless of size, are always alert and active when they are healthy. If your pig seems lethargic and has a dull look in its eyes, then you should ask questions as to why. Don't risk choosing a different piglet from the same litter since if one is ill, the others could be as well and just not as sick at that point.

- *Moist Nose:* Along with being active and having bright eyes, the piglets should have moist noses. If they are dry and cracked, then they could be suffering from a serious illness.

- *Good Coat:* While they don't have a coat like we expect in most pets, pigs do have some hair and even those that don't should have good skin that is shiny and not dry or cracked. It should also not appear dull.

- *Tight Curled Tails:* With the exception of breeds with a straight tail, a healthy piglet should have a nice, tightly curled tail.

- *Good shape:* When you are looking at the piglets, make sure that they have a good shape to them. A pig should have a long body that has a slightly arched back. They should have a wide chest and while their sides should be slightly rounded, they should not be overweight. You should still be able to feel the ribs when you touch the sides of the pig.

- *Well Formed Teats:* Although you may not even think of looking at this, it is important for your pig to have 12 to 14 teats, which are the nipples that run along your piglet's belly, regardless of whether they are male or female. The teats should be well shaped and they should be evenly distributed. If there are fewer teats or they look misshapen, than may be an indicator of some genetic problems the piglet may have.

- *Temperament:* It is important to always check the temperament of your individual piglet whenever you go to see it. If it is showing any signs of aggressive behaviour to the other piglets, or seems to be overly skittish and wild, then you should choose a different piglet from the litter.

In the end, it is all a personal choice and while you may have a preferred colour and gender, it is important that you never choose a piglet based on those two traits. A happy and healthy life with your pet is much more important than the colour they are.

Multiple Pigs or Not

The last thing I would like to look at in this chapter is whether or not you should own multiple micro pigs. If you are interested in breeding pigs, which I will go over at the end of this book, then chances are you will need to own more than one. However, if you are looking for a micro pig to be your pet, then you may simply want to choose one.

As with anything, there are pros and cons of owning two micro pigs at a time but it boils down to how much work do you want to do. Since micro pigs are a social creature, they do much better in homes where they can be with more than one pig. They generally keep each other company and are less destructive since they have another pig to keep them entertained.

However, there are a number of issues that may arise with having two or more pigs. Generally, pigs like to have a hierarchy in the home and they will fight for dominance in the house. One will eventually become the boss pig and they may bully or fight the other pig. They will usually jostle for position during meal times and this can lead to a quite a mess.

In the end, it is really about how much time you have. Two pigs means even more chores and while they do keep each other entertained, they do need the same amount of interaction and love that you would give one.

Chapter Five: Bringing Your Micro Pig Home

Now that you have chosen your breeder and subsequently your piglet, it is time to start getting ready to bring your piglet home. First, it is important to note that there is a lot more involved concerning bringing your piglet home. There are permits to get and you will also need to set up both an outdoor and an indoor space for your piglet.

In this chapter, I will go over everything you need to get your house ready for your micro piglet and also how to make the journey from the farm to your home as stress free as possible.

The Permits

Before you do anything else, you need to sit down and start researching your area. This is imperative if you live in a town or city where there are restrictions on owning an exotic pet or farm animal. Some cities have banned micro pigs completely and if this is the case, it is better for you to know before you actually choose a piglet.

Every country is different; however, most need certain licenses, which I will outline below for you to go over. Make sure you have these permits and licences before you pick up your micro pig.

- **CPH (County Parish Holding):** This is a number that is issued to any owner of a pig, whether it is a micro pig or not and can be purchased from a Rural Payments Agency. It is important to remember that different countries have different policies but most need all pigs to have a number where they can be tracked in the event of a disease outbreak. When you get your number, you will be asked to give your address, phone number and you will also need to list how many pigs you will be owning. A micro pig breeder will not release a pig into your care until you have the original paperwork stating that you have your CPH number.

- **Herd Number:** This actually is a number that is issued to you after you bring your piglet home. At that time, you will need to make a call to your local animal health department and let them know that you now have a pig on your property. They will issue you a herd number, which will need to be marked on your pig, whether it is with an ear tag, a tattoo or a temporary tattoo, if you wish to take your pig off of your property.

- *Pig Walking License:* When you have a pet pig, one thing that you will want to do is take him or her for a walk. Unfortunately, it is not as simple as putting a leash on and heading out. Pigs need to have a special license to be walked anywhere off of their property. Like the herding number, the pig walking license is issued by your local animal health department and does take some time to be done. Generally, when you are applying for your license, you do have to give a proposed walking path that you will be taking. Health officials will ascertain whether the route is safe for your pig and for other animals or whether there are health risks present. If there are health risks, an alternate route will be suggested, however, occasionally, the license is not issued if there are too many health risks. Be aware that simply because you are applying for a walking permit does not mean that you will get one.

When you bring your micro pig home, you will have to fill out a moving form and there are a number of steps to be taken to ensure that your micro pig is transported safely. While it does fall under permits and licensing, I will discuss it separately later in this chapter.

Preparing your Home

Now that you have prepared the paperwork you will need to own your own micro pig, it is time to start getting your home ready for your pig. This can be a bit of a challenge because micro pigs are still a fairly new animal for a house pet and it can be difficult to figure out what type of space you will need to provide for your pig.

One thing to remember is that a micro pig is still a pig, regardless of how small they may be. A micro pig needs ample of outdoor space and many breeders recommend that you keep your pigs outside. Of course, that may not be an option for you, especially if you have your heart set on bringing your pig inside.

Personally, I find that pigs are usually good as both indoor and outdoor pets and the perfect compromise is having them spend their time indoors when you are at home or awake and then spend their time outdoors when you cannot be there to watch them.

Because you will need a safe place for your micro pig both indoors and out, we will need to look at the two different areas that you will need to create for your pig. It is very important that you have everything set up before your pig arrives so you do not cause it any more stress than is necessary since pigs can quickly become ill from too much stress.

Setting up your Micro Pig's Room

The first area that we will look at is setting up your home. While you may give your micro pig free reign of your home later on in his life, it is important to start him off in one area until you are finished housetraining him. Pigs prefer to keep their bedding clean so they will try to avoid going to the bathroom near it. This makes things much easier for you if you keep your piglet in one area since he will be less likely to foul it.

I recommend choosing a room where your pig can have some alone time and is not in the thick of family traffic. Usually a laundry room or a mud room makes the ideal setting for this for two reasons. One, the area is usually easy to close off and two, the area is usually easy to clean in case your piglet does have an accident.

If you don't have an area where your piglet can sleep safely, then it is recommended that you purchase a playpen for your piglet to stay in when you cannot keep a close eye on him. Your piglet can sleep in the playpen for the first two weeks.

Even if your piglet is going to be living most of his time outside, if you bring him home at a young age, usually around 8 to 12 weeks, then he should be brought in to sleep to keep him safe and secure. If he gets too cold, he could get very sick so keep him in a warm room for the first few weeks that he is home with you.

When you are setting up your piglet's room, it is important to provide him with a nice clean and comfortable sleeping area. Rugs, blankets and anything that he can burrow in safely is a good choice. Sleeping bags seem to be a perfect choice since they provide plenty of warmth but the slick fabric can help cool your piggy off as well.

Set it up at the far end of the room, away from where you are setting up his litter pan. If you are litter box training your piglet, place his litter box as far from his sleeping area as possible. This will make him more likely to use it since pigs hate to eliminate in their sleep area.

In another corner of the room, away from both the bedding and the potty area, set up his food and water dishes. This will give him enough space between the three most important parts of your pig's room. Make sure that the room is set up away from any drafts since a piglet is susceptible to getting sick during those first few weeks.

The final part that you should put in your pig's room is a crate. One of the things that I recommend is to place the feeding dishes in or near the crate so your pig becomes familiar with being inside a crate. By having the feeding area close or in the crate, your pig won't feel any unnecessary stress when he has to travel in the crate. It will be a familiar place that your pig will be happy to go into.

Pig Proofing Your Home

Hopefully, when you set up your pig's room, you look for the various treats that your pig will try to swallow. Get down on your hands and knees and look around the room at his level. Remove any little bits of debris that would be tempting to put in his mouth.

Anything that you can find should be removed since he will eat it. Things like small toys, food, clothing, shoes, electronics; basically, everything and anything that would look interesting to a pig. Take any wires or cords and tie them up and place them out of reach of your piglet. Trust me, as he begins to explore his new home, his mouth will be busy tasting everything, including furniture.

Remember that your piglet will be exploring everything so it is important that you have safety locks on any low cupboards. It may seem surprising but a pig can get into just about anything if they smell something that seems extra tasty.

Once you have everything picked up out of reach of your piglet, look at the surfaces that your pig has to walk on. Generally, pigs have a very difficult time walking on slick surfaces such as tile or hardwood and this can lead to your micro pig being injured when he slides on the floor. Instead of keeping him out of rooms, temporarily cover surfaces with throw rugs that can be lifted up later. In general, the older your pig gets, the better he'll be able to navigate those slick floors.

Stairs don't often present a problem for younger pigs, however, the larger your pig gets, the more difficulty he will have getting up and down the stairs, especially if he starts getting some weight on him. Instead of worrying about it later in life, I would recommend putting gates up around stairs and if you need to go up and down stairs to get outside, I would recommend putting up some type of ramp for your pig.

Lastly, to avoid broken glass in your piglet's room, only use metal bowls for feeding and watering. Your pig won't break it by pushing it around and they also won't be able to chew the plastic away. Also, the metal bowls can be purchased with a slip free surface to keep your pig from pushing it all over your house.

The main key to getting your house prepared for your piglet and keeping it safe is to scour every surface you can that your pig will be able to reach. Pigs are very inquisitive creatures and they will be on a constant search for something interesting to chew on.

Creating a Pig Pen

Since micro pigs need ample time outdoors, it is important to have a safe area for your pet pig to go when they are outside. You should never simply put your pig in the garden and then leave him since this is not a secure area by any means.

Again, pigs are very inquisitive and their snout is always on a lookout for something interesting to root up. Unfortunately, this rooting can take them to the fence line and your micro pig will quickly learn how to get out of their yard. For this reason, it is important to have a separate pig pen area for your micro pig whenever he is out in the garden without you.

The first thing for any pig pen, obviously, is a fence. Never use a simple wooden fence unless it is flush with the ground and the nails are rust proof to prevent loosening of the boards. The idea is to have a fence that is over 4 feet (1.22 meters) high and is buried into the ground about a foot down (.31 meters). This serves two purposes. First, the fence can't be rooted up very easily by your micro pig, and two, most predators won't be able to dig under the fence to get at your pig.

Generally, an enclosure for a standard pig should be about 8 feet (2.44 meters) by 16 feet (4.88 meters), however, micro pigs can have a slightly smaller space for a pig pen, however, it shouldn't be that much smaller. A pig pen should not be fenced in with mesh since a pig can chew the mesh to bits and will quickly get out of the pen. Instead, purchase hog panels since they are designed specifically for pigs to prevent them from escaping. If you are not familiar with how to install hog panels, search the web for instructions.

In addition to strong fencing, it is important to have a shelter for your micro pig, whether he will be sleeping outside or not. The shelter should be long and wide enough for the micro pig to turn around in but it does not have to be high, unless you want to be able to crawl inside with the pig.

Usually, a wooden structure with a floor, walls and a roof, similar to a dog house, is all that is needed, however, any wooden structures should have mesh wiring over it to prevent the pig from chewing the wood of the shelter.

Inside the shelter, place amble bedding to keep him warm. Straw is a good bedding to have in the shelter since it provides ample warmth, however, wood chips are usually much easier for clean up.

In addition to bedding, actually look at where your shelter is in the garden. Make sure the shelter gets plenty of direct sunlight and also test it to make sure there are not a lot of drafts throughout the shelter. The more warmth your piglet has, the happier he will be.

The last thing that you should do is keep a feeding trough set up in the corner of your pig pen and to also provide them with a sturdy water bucket. Pigs need plenty of food and water in a day so make sure that your pig has access to both when he is outside.

Although it may be tempting to make the shelter and the pig pen reflects the size of your piglet, it is much better if you take the time to make it large enough for an adult micro pig since this will save you both time and money in the long run. It will also reduce the amount of stress your pig will have since he doesn't have to reacquaint himself with a larger space.

Moving your Micro Pig

When it comes to bringing your pig home, there are a few extra steps that you will need to take besides simply loading him into the car and driving home.

In most countries, pigs cannot be moved without proper licences and it is important to check your local health unit to find out what you need to move your pig and how the pig should be moved.

As you know, before you do anything, you will need to have the County Parish Holding number. This should be issued before the pig is brought home and it will help keep track of the pig and any possible outbreak of disease that can occur.

Once you have that, you can get a movement document. It can be different depending on the country you live in, but in the UK, it should be the AML2, which is a moving form.

When you have that, you can bring your pig home. It is important to realize that once you move your pig, you will need to keep him or her on your premise for a specific number of days depending on where you live. For most places, a standard 20 days are needed where your pig cannot leave the premises of your home.

Outside of a walking permit, which I have gone over already, if you plan on taking your pig anywhere, you will need to fill out the AML2 again to highlight where you pig will be travelling to and how long he will be staying in that location.

Outside of the paperwork, there are a few other things that you should remember about moving your pig so that he has the most success with coming into his new environment.

On the day of the move, you should make sure that you have a secure crate for travelling. This can be a box; however, I would recommend that you use a pet carrier so that you know there is no risk of your piglet getting out of the box.

Make sure you put in plenty of straw for bedding so that your piglet is comfortable and will have minimal stress during the travel. If you are going a long distance, have water available for him but I don't recommend placing it into the crate with him since it can be tipped over and the straw will become uncomfortable.

If you are looking at a very long trip to bring your piglet home, then it is important to bring along some food with you as well. He may not want to eat when you are travelling, but it is important to offer it to him just in case.

Remember when you are travelling that you should never take your piglet out on the road. The permits only allow for the pig to move from the breeder's to the pig's new home and you can face serious fines as well as the loss of your new piglet.

When you are travelling, it is important to place the carrier in a secure area in the car so it won't move around if you happen to stop quickly.

Lastly, always make sure that your pig is not in direct sunlight. Remember that they can get overheated very easily and sun coming through a car window can be torturous for your pig.

In general, piglets do very well travelling and since they don't like to go to the bathroom in their sleeping area, they are not likely to go to the bathroom in their crate during the car ride.

Arriving Home

As I have mentioned already, when you first arrive home with your micro pig, you will need to keep him on the premise for the first 20 to 30 days. Make sure that you are sure of the time period you have to wait and never take your piglet out visiting before that time period, even if you get a walking permit.

When you arrive home, it is important to let your piglet settle into the new surroundings. He will be very nervous, especially since he has been taken from his siblings and mom. There won't be a lot of bonding right away so don't worry about your piglet not wanting to be around you. Simply give him time to settle in.

Take him into his "space" and open the crate so he can come out on his own. Never pull him out since this will cause more harm than good. Once you have opened his crate, simply walk away and allow him to explore things on his own.

Don't leave the room but settle down close at hand at first, making sure that you don't force contact with your piglet. Put out food and water for him and try to offer the food to entice him towards you.

Spend as much time as you can in his room during the first few days that he has arrived home, again, never forcing contact but taking time to stroke him when he walks by. Use food to gain his trust and keep everything calm and quiet for him.

Don't introduce him to your other pets during the first few days since you will want him to gain trust with you before you bring in another source of possible stress. People in the family can come into the room with you as your piglet becomes more comfortable in his new surroundings but make sure they follow the same rules that you are. Stay quiet and let the piglet get used to people on his own terms.

It may be better to have children wait a few days before you bring them into the room since they can frighten the piglet very easily through their excitement.

After a few days, your piglet will become more confident in his environment and will start to bond with you and the people that you bring into the room. It does take patience and it is very important to reduce the number of stressors that could hinder the bonding process with your pig.

Shopping List for your Pig

When it comes to supplies, you won't need that much for your pig. They are not like other pets that need a complicated set up and other than a nice place to sleep and an outdoor run, a micro pig is happy to lay his snout anywhere.

Still, you will need a few things and I have created a short list of all the items you will need for your pig.

Travel Crate: This is important for bringing your micro pig home; however, I would also recommend using it as a place for your pig to sleep when he is inside. This will give him somewhere comfortable to go and you can remove the door from the crate so there is no risk of him getting locked inside. Make sure that you purchase the crate to the size you think he will reach as an adult since there is no point spending the extra cost on a different crate for each growth spurt.

Food and Water Dishes: It is important to purchase food and water dishes for both indoors and outdoors for you pig. Try to find ones that are not easy to tip but are low to the ground so it is easier for your pig to reach. Many pigs like to tip over their food dishes so make sure you purchase one that is difficult to do so.

Harness: Although some people love a collar on a pig, it is much safer for your pig if you use a harness that goes around his chest. This is simply for walks and you will need to purchase new ones as your micro pig grows.

Leash: A standard 6 foot (1.83 meters) leash is important to have for walks and I would keep it limited to flat leashes made from nylon or leather. Never use a chain leash with a pig.

Straw: Straw or any other type of bedding will be needed for your piglet. There are different kinds of bedding and it is really what you prefer. I have found that straw is fine and it keeps your pig nice and warm as well as comfortable. It is also the less expensive option.

Shelter for Outdoors: You can purchase a shelter for your pig or you can make one on your own but you should have somewhere for your pig to get out of the heat or any other increment weather.

Litter Box: Some pigs can learn to use a litter box, which I will go over later in this book, however, even if you aren't litter training your pig, it may be a good idea to have one available for your piglet.

Secure Fencing: When your pig is outside, it is important to have secure fencing for him. Remember to follow the guidelines set out in getting ready for your pig.

Treats: Just like dogs, micro pigs can learn very easily if they are given treats as an incentive. Be sure to have a few high quality pig treats available for when your piglet comes home.

And that is about all you need to start your life with your new piglet. If you are keeping him inside, you should get a few baby gates to keep him away from stairs and out of rooms that you don't want him in.

Chapter Six: Socializing your Micro Pig

One area that is very important to having a well rounded micro pig is socialization. A micro pig needs to be introduced to a number of stimuli and people so that they are confident and healthy adult pigs.

In this chapter, I will go over the several areas of socialization including bonding with your piglet and introducing your piglet to other animals and people.

Bonding with your Piglet

Although I have touched on bonding with your piglet slightly in the last chapter, I want to look at it specifically since the bonding process is very important to ensure that you have a good relationship with your pig.

The first thing that I want to stress is that every piglet is different. They all have different personalities and some may adjust better to humans than others. Each breed of micro pig or pet pig has a different temperament and they may take less time or more time to bond.

It is important to really take the advice of your piglet's breeder. He or she will understand the breed of pig that you are purchasing and can give you many helpful tips to help the bonding process.

The key to bonding with your micro pig is socialization. It is important to choose a breeder that provides a lot of hands on interaction with the piglets while they are young to ensure that they are more trusting of humans.

When they arrive home, it is important to realize as the owner that the piglet will need to spend time adjusting before you begin the bonding process. Piglets are usually very fearful, naturally so, and even one that has been properly socialized by the breeder, will still suffer from this fearfulness at the new situation.

Although it may be exciting to jump into training and life as usual, it is imperative that you don't. Instead, simply give the pig a few days to adjust before you start expecting behavior from him.

Bonding is usually a slow process so be prepared for it to take a few days or even a few weeks. It is important to spend time with your piglet on a daily basis and to follow a series of steps to ensure that your piglet becomes accustomed to you.

Day One:

The first day is always the most stressful for your piglet and it is best if you simply bring him home and then set him up in his room.

Once he is relaxed enough, go in and sit down on the floor with him. Make sure that you sit away from him and that you allow your micro pig to explore the room without interfering.

When he is calm, take out a small treat and place it on the floor near you. Make sure it is about an arm's length away so your piglet doesn't have to get too close. Don't talk to him at first, just let him discover the food.

When he starts eating the food, quietly praise him but don't reach for him unless he seems very calm. Do this for about 15 minutes, several times during the first day.

Day Two:

Like the first day, you should enter the room quietly and simply sit down on the floor. Watch your micro pig and see if he is curious about you at all. Piglets can be quite curious so if he shows interest, just let him explore without reaching for him, since this could startle him.

If he has no interest, place the treat out beside you again. This time, you can move it slightly closer but make sure you watch your piglet's body language to find out if he is comfortable with getting it.

Again, talk quietly to him when he finds the food and if he seems calm, you can gently stroke him, but don't rush contact if you feel that he is stressed by it.

The second day is a good time to start having members of your family come into the room. Adults can go into the room on their own, as long as they follow the bonding steps, but children should never be left alone. Bring in something quiet for them to do with you while the piglet moves around them.

Day Three:

Hopefully, by day three, you should be starting your bond with your piglet. He should be comfortable with your presence and may even come and sniff at you when you get into the room.

Again, start by sitting but move the food closer towards you when you go to feed your piglet. If you can entice him to take the food from your hand, day three is a good time to do so.

When he does take the food, try scratching your piglet under his chin with your fingertips or gently bring your other hand up to his side. Do not bring it down over top of your piglet since this can startle him.

As you pet you piglet, watch his reaction. If he appears to be very nervous and resists your contact, simply wait until the next day to try again. Remember that this can be a very slow process.

It is important when you are with your piglet that you do not always offer him food. Spend five or ten minutes in the room simply sitting with him and then the next time offer him a treat. If you over treat him, your piglet will always demand food from you whenever he sees you.

Day Four:

Day four is very similar to day three where you simply entice your piglet over to you and try to touch him and pet him. Make sure that you continue to use a soft tone and that you do not pick your piglet up, no matter how tempting it is.

Pigs prefer to have all four feet on the ground and it can become very stressful for your piglet if you are trying to pick him up and snuggle with him.

Once he becomes accustomed to you, it is okay to try to get him to come and sit on your lap. This has to be done very slowly and it is better to take a blanket that he has been using for a bed and place it near you.

After a few days, you can begin to move the blanket between your legs so that your piglet is sitting on the floor between you. This is a sign that your micro pig is starting to trust you and will soon be nestled in your lap.

In addition to you being with your pig, you can start to expand his world a bit more. During the first few days, it is better to keep him confined to his room; however, on day four, you can open up an additional room for him. Remember to keep things calm for your piglet when he goes into the new room and take the time to let him explore on his own. If you have other pets, make sure that they do not have access to your piglet when they are first exploring a new room since it can lead to a very stressful and potentially threatening situation.

Day Five:

During the fifth day, you can begin to handle your piglet more if he is becoming more accustomed to you. Instead of simply scratching him when you are enticing him with food, try doing so when you don't have food in hand.

If he is receptive to being handled, move him into your lap and allow him to lie down. Make sure you put his blanket into your lap as well. Your piglet will feel more comfortable if there is something familiar there when you do.

Continue to talk to him throughout the process so your piglet becomes familiar with you and begins to build that bond that you are hoping for.

The process should continue on for several days or weeks, again, make sure that you move slowly from one step to the next until your piglet is comfortable. If he seems resistant to a step, take your time to introduce it.

Once your piglet is comfortable in your lap, you can move to putting your arms around him and then slowly lifting him up and cradling in your arms. It is very important that you do this slowly and it may take several weeks before you are able to pick him up without him becoming stressed.

A sure sign of your pig becoming stressed is when he begins squealing. When he does this, make sure that he is squealing because of severe stress. If it is more of a complaint over being handled and not a fear driven response, work through the squeal, trying to comfort him with your voice. If he is squealing because of stress, and trust me, you will be able to notice the difference, set him down.

The main reason why you shouldn't do this when he is simply complaining is because a piglet will learn quickly that a little bit of squealing will get him what he wants; all four feet on the ground, and it will create a habit for your piglet throughout his life.

It is important to properly hold your piglet when you are lifting him to reduce the amount of stress that he is feeling. Always hold him in the cradle of your arm. Place your one arm around your piglet's neck and chest so that his front legs are behind your arm while your other arm is around his rump and your hand is pressed against his side and he should be pressed against you. By cradling him this way, you will make him feel secure and less likely to struggle and squeal while you hold him.

During the period that you are bonding with your piglet, it is important to take things very slowly. Never rush and never rely solely on food to get your micro pig's attention. Don't always sit down when you are in the room. Your piglet will need to get used to you moving around him and doing things so spend time working in the room, either cleaning up his room or doing something for yourself with your piglet under foot.

Lastly, never begin training your piglet until you have started the bonding process and your micro pig is comfortable with you. If you start too early, you can end up ruining the bond that you have been trying so hard to create.

Introducing Your Micro Pig to Other Pets

One thing that I have stressed throughout this chapter is that it is very frightening for a piglet when he arrives at a new home. Things need to be controlled to keep his stress to a minimum and to help with the bond that you have.

Unfortunately, when you have another pet, some of your control may slip away, especially if the animal is sniffing and worrying at the door where your piglet is.

One thing to keep in mind is that pigs tend to be dominant and they may become the boss pig of the other animals. This is not something that you can control since animals in the home establish their own hierarchy regardless of what their humans want.

When you are introducing your piglet to other animals in the home, do so gradually. Wait until your piglet is used to the surroundings and then allow your other pets to sniff around the door. The piglet will become accustomed to the noises and smells from behind the door and your other pets may start to lose interest in what they smell.

When your piglet seems calm, place a baby gate up so your animals can see each other through the gate. Let the piglet become comfortable with the open door first but once he is, start bringing your other pet into the space and allowing the animals to sniff each other through the gate.

Continue this for a few days and then allow the animals to be in the same room. If you have a dog, keep him on a leash and in a down stay while the piglet moves around him. Let the piglet initiate the contact and then allow the dog the opportunity to sniff the pig.

Cats can be different since they will often meet new animals on their own terms. Allow your cat to sit up high and watch the piglet but keep close to avoid any confrontations that could startle your micro pig.

Limit the amount of access they have to each other for the first few days and then start expanding the time that they spend together. It is important that you never leave two animals together alone until they can be trusted completely with each other.

Introducing Your Micro Pig to People

I have touched on this in bonding but your micro pig will be coming into contact with more than just the people in their family. He will need to get used to being approached by people that don't know him and he will need to get used to people coming into the house.

While much of the socialization during the first few weeks will be centered around your home, it is important to start inviting people into your home to meet your new piglet.

Since the first 20 to 30 days will be spent at home with your pig, it is important to start bringing people into the house after the first week or week and a half after your piglet arrives. Never have them come over the day you bring your piglet home since this can lead to severe stress for your micro pig.

Start with one person and have them come in and meet the pig in the same manner that you bonded with him. Make sure they sit on the floor and let the piglet come and greet them on his own terms.

Give them a few treats to tempt the piglet with and then have them scratch the piglet being the ears or on the side in a calm manner. If the piglet seems upset by the contact, simply have the person sit back and ignore the piglet.

If they prefer not to sit on the floor, simply have them sit down on a chair and wait for the piglet to come to them. Make sure that they reach down and out instead of directly over the pig when they go to pet him since it can startle him if they reach directly down from above.

Once your piglet gets used to one person, invite two people to come over and again, have them sit down in the chairs and repeat the process. Continue to do this, adding more people to the group until your piglet is comfortable with meeting new people.

Chapter Seven: Nutrition and Your Micro Pig

Now that your micro pig is home and you have begun socializing it, you may be wondering what, exactly, does a micro pig eat.

Before you begin purchasing treats for your micro pig, it is important to stress that while pigs are often described as the disposal unit of the animal world, they should never live off of leftovers and "slop," which is leftover food. There are foods that can be harmful to your pig, which can be found in slop and there are laws that prohibit the feeding a pet pig a diet of only leftovers.

Despite the laws, feeding a micro pig in this manner is bad for his health and will result in many costly vet visits and may even shorten the lifespan of your pig.

While we can look at food in the whole, I find that it is much easier to look at in terms of daily meals, training treats, and the occasional snack that your micro pig will be receiving.

Daily Meals for Your Micro Pig

Before we even look at the food, there is one thing that I need to stress for you, never, and I mean never, feed your piglet when he is squealing. For the same reason that you should avoid putting him down when he is squealing slightly, a micro pig will quickly learn that the more fuss he makes, the faster you will feed him.

Instead, wait until he has stopped squealing to put down his food or simply feed him in a different room and then bring him in once the food is out. Trust me; giving in to a squealing pig will only make things worse for you in the long run.

When you are choosing a food for your micro pig, it is important to consider the following:

Quality: Don't choose the least expensive food and look for one that has a healthy range of grains, fruits and vegetables. Never use a pig food that contains traces of meat since it is not healthy for them, despite the fact that pigs are omnivores and will eat both meat and plants.

High Fibre: Although your pig will love all the extras, it is important to find a feed that is high in fibre for optimal health in your pig.

Vegetables: Although I already touched on this, you should look for a food that makes up a large percentage of your pig's daily calories in vegetables. Generally, 25% of your pig's diet should consist of vegetables.

Low Calorie: Find a food that has a low calorie score for your pig since you do not want him gaining weight too quickly. Pigs generally eat a lot of food throughout the day, simply from rooting, so don't worry about your pig getting enough calories.

When it comes to things to avoid in your pig food, there are a few things and I just want to highlight them briefly.

Fat: Some fat is good but it shouldn't make up more than 15% of your pig's diet. Avoid any food that has a high fat content and also make sure that it is free of animal fats, since this can lead to health problems in your micro pig.

Salt: Another ingredient that can lead to serious health risks in your micro pig, check the ingredients list for any salt or salt by-product in the food.

Enriched: Okay, we want to choose foods that are enriched in good ways but you should avoid any foods that are enriched for growth. These foods are designed for rapid weight gain and are usually used in pig farms for meat since it will ensure the pigs grow quickly. Foods to avoid are ones that say starter, grower or breeder since these are high in fats and calories and will increase your pig's growth rate.

Pet Food: Although you will need to purchase a food that is designed for pet pigs, never feed your micro pig dog food or cat food. In fact, never feed him any type of pet food that does not specifically say pig food since they do not have the nutritional values that a pig needs for a healthy life.

The best food for your piglet is one that is designed for pet pigs and I would recommend taking the advice of the brand from your veterinarian or from your pig's breeder. There are a number that are available commercially through many pet food suppliers and online, however, they are only available in certain countries so make sure to check what is available for you.

Feeding your Micro Pig

When it comes to daily meals, it may seem like your micro pig needs plenty of food. Pigs are, after all, known for their fat so it may seem like you need to feed them a lot of food during the day.

Generally, a micro pig will root around for food throughout the day and will spend some of his day eating grass. By constantly eating, your micro pig will get all of the calories that he needs and then some. It is important to note before you put any food out for your pig that the guidelines on most commercial pig foods are incorrect for micro pigs.

In general, you should only feed your pig about 2 to 2.5% of his body weight per day. This usually equals about ½ cup of food for every 25 pounds of pig. Your pig should have one meal per day and the rest of his calories should be broken up into grazing and treats. Young piglets can be fed a starter food for extra calories; however, they should be weaned from starter food by the time they are 3 months of age.

In addition to his pig food, your pig should be given plenty of opportunity to graze in soil and grass. This will make sure that he has the proper calorie intake and he will also get a good source of selenium, which pigs often have a deficiency in. If your pig does not have access to a good area of grass and soil, you should check with your veterinarian for mineral supplements.

When you are feeding your micro pig, make sure that you take the time to check his weight on a regular basis. You will not have to weigh him constantly but look at his face and check for heavy wrinkles around the head. Check the amount of fat around his hips. The general rule is if there are excess wrinkles on the face and you can't feel your pig's hips, then your micro pig is obese and needs to go on a diet.

Although you can split your pig's meals up into two meals, I find that it is better to allow your pig to graze through the morning and then feed him in the afternoon. This ensures that he is getting enough food and that he isn't getting too much. Remember that pigs will not stop eating, even if they don't feel hungry.

Treats and Snacks for your Micro Pig

Treats are wonderful for your micro pig and they are perfect for use in positive reinforcement training, which we will get into in the next section.

When you are giving treats, there are a few things that you need to remember for your pig.

1. Consider them in your pig's daily calorie intake. Remember that treats can add calories to your pig's diet and they can lead to your pig becoming obese. Don't overfeed your pig treats since this can cause many health problems.

2. Limit the number of treats per day. While we love to give our pets treats, pigs can be horrible beggars and the more treats you give them, the worse they will beg.

3. Never feed from the cupboard or the fridge. The main reason for this is because a pig is a very intelligent animal, especially where food is concerned. If your pig learns that food can be found in a low cupboard or the fridge, he will go and get it himself whenever he wants. And trust me, a pig can learn how to pry open a fridge door very quickly.

4. Keep them small. A treat should be small in quantity. A piece of celery or a carrot as opposed to a whole bushel of carrots. A small piece of cheese, no bigger than your index finger, instead of a huge slice the size of your palm. If you feed large treats, your pig will become obese very quickly.

Generally, a micro pig can eat just about anything when it comes to treats and should receive about 25% of their daily food in vegetables and it works best if you provide those vegetables in snack form. Bury them in a sandbox for your pig to root out to entertain his mind and to also get him the vegetables that you need.

Treats and snacks for your pig can be:

Vegetables: Any type of vegetable is good for your micro pig. I recommend that you avoid vegetables for training treats since they are not chewed easily and will disrupt the training session.

Fruit: Fruit is always a big hit with micro pigs and this is usually because they are sweet. In fact, they can enjoy fruit so much that they avoid eating their veggies. Fruit should be given less frequently as snacks and softer fruit can be the perfect option for a training treat. Make sure that you make them bite sized morsels for training if you do use them.

Cereals: Another great training treat, cereal is just the right size and often has the added benefit of providing your pig with more fibre. In addition to treats, adding a little bran to your pig's feed will give him extra fibre through the day, which is always beneficial.

Cheese: Although it should be given in moderation, I have found that micro pigs love cheese. This should be something that you use for training and should only be given in small amounts when you do. Make sure you cut them into bite sized pieces for training.

Alfalfa: Alfalfa is a good source of fibre and greens and I would recommend adding them to your pig's daily diet.

When it comes to the individual pigs, you will find that some foods are his favorite and some are not. Just try different foods to determine what really gets him interested in performing for the tricks. Once you have a list, try and add new treats for your pig and make sure that you mix it up a bit to add a little variety for your pig.

One thing that I should mention is that there are some foods that should be avoided including:

- *Chocolate:* Although it is not confirmed, chocolate has been linked to several health risks for your pig. Even if it isn't deadly, it has a large amount of sugar in it, which can lead to obesity in your pig.

- *Potatoes:* Any type of potato from sweet to new are not good for pigs since they are high in starch and calories and can lead to obesity.

- **Corn:** Like fruit, corn has a lot of fructose in it and can lead to weight and health problems in your pig.

- **Tomatoes:** The high level of acid found in tomatoes are not recommended for pigs.

- **Spinach:** While it is high in vitamins, spinach is also high in sodium and salt should be avoided with your pig's diet.

- **Candy:** There is nothing that can be gained from giving a pig candy and your pig may start to demand candy if you do offer it to him. Extra calories, sugars and a number of other factors that are present in candy are not healthy for your pig at all.

Other than the foods listed above, most foods are okay for pigs and where you are in doubt, simply avoid it. Your pig is not going to miss something if he has never had it in the first place.

When it comes to feeding your micro pig, the goal is to provide him with enough treats to help with his calories, give him plenty of grazing time and then give him the rest of his calorie intake in a small amount of food.

Regardless of how or what you are feeding your pig, it is imperative that he has a constant supply of fresh water. It may be tempting to offer your pig something other than water, such as fruit juice; however, if you make a habit of offering them something besides water, they will begin to demand it and will turn their snouts up at water.

Chapter Eight: Training Your Micro Pig

Training a micro pig is very similar to training a dog. They are usually very intelligent and they are food motivated so positive reinforcement will have the best results with training.

When it comes to commands, a micro pig can learn most of the basic commands that a dog can learn. They can be quite skilled at a number of tricks and some have even been taught how to be agility pigs.

The main point of training is to simply find a treat that your micro pig loves and then make him work for it. Once he understands that work equals food, he will be more than willing to learn for you.

In this chapter, we will be going over a few basic commands that you can teach your micro pig and will also cover housetraining and leash training your pig.

Basic Commands

Although your pig will try to rule the home, it is important for you to teach him basic commands so he learns that you are the boss in the house.

One thing that I want to stress with treating during training is that you should never give a treat when your pig is squealing. The reason for this is simply because he will learn that squealing means food and will forget that listening was the reason he got it in the first place.

Sit

Sit is very simple to teach and I would recommend that you teach it where your pig will end up backing into a wall. If you do it in an open space, your pig

will just continue to move backwards to see the treat.

Start with the pig standing in front of you with his back end pointed towards the wall. Hold a treat in your hand and say, "Sit, pig." Bring the treat up and over his head so he has to sit to be able to follow it.

When his bottom hits the ground, say, "Good sit, pig," and then give him the treat. Repeat until he will sit without you guiding him into the sit.

Down

Place your pig into a sit and say, "Down, pig," before you lower the treat down to the ground and away from the pig so he has to slip down to get at the treat.

Once he is in the position, say, "Good down, pig," and treat him. Give him a few rubs to let him know that being down is a great place to be.

Come

A very easy command to train if you have food, your pig may not always come when you don't have food. It can take a bit of time but eventually your pig will learn that come results in some type of reward, whether from you praising him or you feeding him.

Wait until your pig is away from you and then crouch down to his level. Put out the treat and begin calling him, "Come, pig". Get his attention by waving the food out and when he comes running up to get the food, say, "Good come, pig," before giving him the treat.

When you teach come, make sure that you touch him so he learns that you may be calling him to do some type of handling. If you don't touch him, he may learn to avoid you when he comes and this is not what you want.

As you can see, training a micro pig is very similar to training a dog and uses the same techniques and commands. The main point is to use food to lure your pig into the command and for reward. You should never begin training your micro pig until you have established a bond with him.

Leash Training

Harness training your pig can be easy or difficult and it really comes down to how you approach it with your pig. If you start before your pig has begun to trust you, then it will cause problems with leash training and your micro pig may never take to it fully.

Before you start leash training your pig, you really need to know that he is ready for it. Start by touching his ears and head and then his body. If he is fine with you touching him, then he is ready to start learning how to walk on the leash. If he isn't, then you will need to return to the socialization chapter in this book and continue on in with the process of socializing and building a bond with your pig.

When he is ready to wear a harness, it is very important that you do not force him to wear it. Start by showing him the harness and allow him to sniff and explore it on his own. Talk to him soothingly as he does so he learns that he doesn't need to be afraid of the harness.

When he becomes familiar with it, touch it to his body gently. Do not put it on but only get him used to the feel of it on his skin. If he shies away from it, stop for the day and try again the next day.

If you can touch him with the harness without frightening him, it is time to put it on. The best type of harness to use for a micro pig is an H-style harness where the harness is fastened around his neck and his stomach instead of having to have a loop slide over his ears and face.

Place food on the ground to distract your micro pig and then slowly place the harness on him. Soothe him with your voice as you fasten it and then sit back. If he starts to panic, try to get his attention with a treat and try to avoid taking the harness off. If he becomes terrified, take the harness off and try again on a different day.

Continue to get your pig used to the harness over the course of the week until he becomes very comfortable with having it put on and with wearing it for a short period of time.

When he is, you can place the lead onto the harness. This is often when your pig will have the biggest fight since this means that he is being restrained, which is stressful for a pig.

Instead of holding the leash, you should simply allow it drag on the ground. Stay close to your pig so it doesn't get caught on anything and give him plenty of treats and praise while he is wearing it.

Repeat this a few times until he is used to the weight and drag of the leash. When he is, pick up the leash and follow him wherever he goes. At this stage, never pull back on the leash but apply a little pit of tension so he knows that he is not restrained but there is something there. Give him plenty of treats and free reign at this point.

Again, leash training is a slow process and you should give your micro pig a few days to adjust to this step of leash training. When he has, you can start to put a little pull on it.

Start by pulling the leash slightly and calling him. As soon as he looks at you, give him a treat and encourage him to move closer to you. Repeat until he is comfortable with this stage.

The next step is to start walking with him on the leash, going in the direction that you want him to go. Start by pulling the leash and then luring him with a treat to take a few steps with you. Give him the treat when he does and lots of praise. Repeat, lengthening the number of steps you take each time.

By this point, your pig will learn that the leash is keeping him close to you and as long as he follows, he is not restrained in any way. You may need to keep treating him for the first few weeks of walks until he learns that he needs to follow and not lead but eventually he will get it.

When you are leash training, it is very important that you do not expose your micro pig to stressful situations. Pigs have very long memories and if they have a negative experience on the leash, they will remember it for life and will never be a great leash walker.

Housetraining Your Micro Pig

Like all pets that you have inside, it is very important to teach a micro pig to do his business outside or in a litter box.

One benefit of a micro pig is that they are usually very clean. Micro pigs will avoid going to the bathroom where they eat or sleep so they can be taught easily that the house is their big bedroom where they should avoid soiling.

Remember, like all training with the micro pig, it should be started slowly and done in slow, gradual steps. If you rush training or bully a micro pig into training, you will find that your pig will shut down and the bond you have been working so hard to establish is destroyed.

Litter Box Training

If you want your pig to use a litter box, then you will need to start by keeping your pig in a confined area instead of giving him access to the rest of the house. This should be followed until your micro pig has been fully litter trained and even then he should never have access to a large section of the house until he is 6 months old or older.

When you are litter box training, make sure that you use a litter box that is big enough for your pig to get in. You will want to have the litter box close to where he sleeps but not too close where he views it as part of his sleeping arrangements.

Start by confining your pig into a small space. Generally, pigs do not go to the bathroom when they are roaming and usually go when they have settled in for the night.

Bring your micro pig over to the litter box every two hours and have him sniff around the litter box and inside it. If it is possible, leave one "pig berry", or pig poop inside the box since the scent will encourage him to go to the bathroom in it again. A pig will not usually use a clean box.

If he doesn't go to the bathroom, don't worry, simply return him to his confined area and then repeat the process in another two hours. When he does go to the bathroom, praise him but never give him a treat for doing it. Remember that going to the bathroom is a natural function and should not be rewarded.

Continue to do this until the pig starts to go to the litter box on his own to use it. Some pigs will learn within a day, while others may take up to a week to learn how to litter train.

It is important during this time to never scold or punish your micro pig for accidents at that time since that can cause more problems than it solves. Simply keep him on a schedule and keep at it, taking him back to the litter box every 2 hours until he learns that that is where he needs to go.

Remember to clean the accidents thoroughly so there is no scent, which will entice him to go in that spot again.

Training to go Outside

It is easier to train your pig to go outside if you have already started him on the litter box. The best way to do this is to simply move the litter box close to the door. Remember to bring him to the litter box the first few times so he knows where it is.

Once he is using the litter box near the door, start to move outside when you see him going to the box. Take him to a spot in the yard where you want him to go to the bathroom and wait until he goes.

If he doesn't, bring him back in and repeat. Again, it is best if you have a "pig berry" in the spot where you want him to go since this will encourage him to go in that spot.

Repeat until he begins to go outside. Some pigs will still need to have a litter box inside, however, if he has access to the backyard and he goes to the door to be let out, you may be able to remove the litter box from the house.

Problem Solving

All pigs have natural instincts that can lead to behavioural problems and while you can only do so much for some things, there are a few ways to problem solve the more annoying behaviours your pig is doing.

Rooting

Rooting is natural for your pig and is when he pushes his snout into something to dig grubs and other treats up. Pigs will root in soil, clothes, hay or anything where they feel there is something to be gained. It is a behaviour that really shouldn't be discouraged, however, if the rooting is becoming destructive, you will need to curb it slightly.

First, make sure that you are providing him with plenty of rooting activities, either in a rooting box or in a sand box. If he has those and he has begun rooting on your legs, then you are going to have to change your habits.

Many pigs will root on people once they learn that they get food from people. This can be very frustrating and it can actually lead to bruises. When your pig roots, place your hand down to block him and say, "No root." Move away from him and do not give him a treat.

You should start giving him treats in a bowl. This will help curb his habit of rooting on you since he never gets food directly from your hand and will turn his rooting to his food dish.

If the rooting becomes uncontrollable, you can use a nose ring. This will help decrease the amount of rooting your micro pig does.

Wallowing

Another natural behaviour, pigs love to wallow in soil and everything else that is cool to their skin. Wallowing is when a pig will dig up and begin to roll and lay in whatever he dug up. It is important for both health and entertainment reasons to provide your pig with ample places to wallow.

Give him a pool to cool off in or a sandbox or mud puddle. By providing him with the proper wallowing places, your pig will avoid wallowing everywhere else.

Biting

Finally, biting is often the result of a pig being fed treats by hand. It is very important to stop giving your pig treats as soon as this starts and to make sure that he works for all of his food. Never give him something simply because he asked or is cute.

You may need to start placing his food and treats in a bowl to prevent biting.

Most pigs can be very docile creatures that simply love being with you but they do need firm rules and training should be a must if you want more than a farm animal sharing your life.

Chapter Nine: Daily Care of Your Micro Pig

Despite the fact that pigs seem to need a lot of care, they are actually fairly sufficient. Provide them with the space that they need, and a pig will usually take care of all his own needs without the help of you.

Thankfully, a pig does enjoy being cared for and it will only strengthen your bond with your pig if you care for him on a daily basis.

In this chapter, I will go over everything that you need to know to ensure that your pig's daily grooming and exercise needs are being met.

Grooming Needs

Although pigs do not seem to have a lot of hair to care for, there is still a fair amount of grooming that needs to be done on a regular basis. It is important to realize that there is a difference between brushing and grooming. Brushing is simply working out the coat while grooming is a word used to describe all of your pig's hygiene needs such as nail trimming, ear cleaning and brushing.

You should expect to groom your pig about 2 or 3 times per week. It should be noted that most micro pig breeds are non-shedding; however, there are some breeds that have a thick coat and will shed. Because of this, you should expect some hair in your house, especially if you have a micro pig breed that has a coat.

To keep your pig at his best, it is recommended that you dedicate 10 minutes to grooming every day and that you start to familiarize your piglet with grooming as soon as he comes home. The better socialized he is with grooming; the more enjoyable grooming will be for both of you.

Brushing

Brushing can be done on a daily basis and it serves two purposes, one is simply that it keeps your pig tidy and will remove any dirt and debris from the hair and two, it will stimulate the blood flow in the skin. Better blood flow means a healthier coat and fewer skin problems.

To brush your pig, work in sections

starting at the top of the neck. Brush down and back in the direction that the hair is going. You do not need to use a heavy brush for this and I would recommend only using a curry comb, which is a round tool that has metal or rubber teeth to catch short hair.

When you brush your micro pig, give soothing sounds and the occasional treat so he begins to see grooming as a positive thing. Make sure to check your pig over for any sores or skin problems as you brush him so you can catch any potential problems early.

Bathing

Bathing only needs to be done when it is absolutely necessary and you will find that pigs are very clean animals. Despite the common belief that pigs will root in their own feces, pigs will avoid feces completely if they have the room to do so.

Pigs will wallow in mud and dirt as a way to cool down and the dust from this will need to be washed off on a regular basis. Still, it is important that you do not over bath your pig since this will lead to dry and flaky skin.

When you bathe your pig, do so in a tub or a bucket that your pig can stand in comfortably. Make sure that you place a mat or a towel down on the bottom of the tub to keep him from slipping and getting hurt.

Fill the tub with water and then drizzle about 2 tbsp of baby oil in to the water. This will help prevent dry skin.

Place your pig into the warm water and hold onto his front legs with one hand. Be sure to soothe him with your voice but keep a hand on his legs at all time to keep control of him.

Sponge the water carefully over your pig starting from the top and working your way down. Make sure that you do not get water into the ears and eyes and try to keep it off of the head.

Once he has been rinsed, work a shampoo onto his skin. The best shampoo to use is a baby shampoo since it is mild and won't be too damaging to his skin.

Rinse the shampoo off and then remove your pig from the bath. Towel him dry and don't allow him to go back outside until he has had the chance to dry completely since he could get a chill.

In between baths, give your pig access to a kiddie pool filled with water. Micro pigs love to play in water and not only will it cool him down but it will also clean him between his baths.

Daily Skin Care

Pigs often have very dry skin and it is not uncommon for them to get dandruff and other skin problems. While they are not prone to fleas, they can be prone to having mites and lice. Because of this, daily skin care is important in keeping your micro pig healthy and happy.

The first step to daily skin care is in taking a quick glance at the skin. Look for any parasites that may be present and also look for any skin problems. Many times, the skin of your micro pig will become very thick and itchy around the ears and legs and this can be very irritating to your pig.

Once you have looked your pig over, treat any of the parasites that you have seen. Make sure you check with your veterinarian to treat lice and mites and that you use what your vet recommends.

If you do not see any parasites, then you can simply follow a regular skin care regime. Pigs can be susceptible to sunburns so it is important to rub sunscreen into his skin every day, even during overcast days.

Use a sunscreen designed for children and make sure that you use one with an SPF of 50 or higher. Avoid any sunscreens with a heavy scent and avoid any that have a lot of parabens and chemicals in it. The more natural the product, the better it is for your micro pig.

When you are using sunscreen, make sure that you apply it to the soft pink areas of the body including the main body. Ears, nose, and feet are at a higher risk of sunburn than other parts of the pig.

In addition to sunscreen, take the time to spray your piglet down with a glycerine solution. Combine 1 part glycerine with 9 parts water and place in a spray bottle. Sprits the solution over your micro pig and allow it to soak into the skin. This will help with keeping the skin soft.

Trimming Hooves

If you are not comfortable with trimming your pig's hooves, then I would recommend that you ask your vet or hire someone to do this for you. 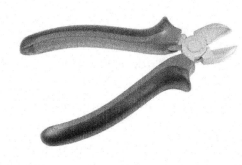 It is important that a pig's hooves be trimmed every few months, although some can go a year between trimming, since improperly groomed hooves will cause your pig to stand and walk improperly, which will lead to joint problems.

To cut your pig's hooves, you will need a diagonal cut mini pliers or spring loaded side cutters. Only use steel cutters since they are sharper and are much easier to clean. You will need a metal nail file that is large enough to be used on pigs.

Before you trim the hooves, it is important to help your pig relax. Start by massaging his body and rubbing his tummy. You should also spend time, whether you are trimming them or not, touching the hooves so he becomes desensitized to it.

Once he is relaxed, you can begin to trim. Take your micro pig's hoof into your hand while he is lying on his side. Place the pliers against the bottom of the hoof and snip away at the flaky parts of the hoof.

Trim the nail until you are close to the smooth, hard part of the nail. Remember to cut back both sides of the nail but don't cut between the toes as this may injure your pig. Round off the sides of the cut.

Once it is cut, take a metal nail file and rub away the sharp edges.

Repeat on all of the hooves and also on the dewclaws. Remember that the hooves should be smooth and should not have any sharp edges.

Ear Cleaning

The last grooming task that you will need to do with your micro pig is keeping his ears clean. Cleaning the ears is very easy to do and it should be done on a weekly or bi-weekly basis.

When you do clean your pig's ears, make sure that you take the time to look inside them. Check for any infections or ear mites so that it can be treated before it becomes a big problem.

Never pour water into your micro pig's ears since this can lead to an ear infection and is very irritating for them. Instead, take a washcloth and dampen it slightly. Hold the ear with one hand and expose the inside of it. With the other, wipe away any dirt, debris and even pig food from the flap and near the ear canal. Never push down into the ear canal since this can damage the ear.

Once it is clean, turn it over and wipe away any dirt from the outside of the ear.

Next, take a small toothbrush and scrub at the dirt that has formed around the base of the ear. There is often a lot of dead skin, food and mud that gets trapped in that spot. Once the dirt has been worked loose, dampen the washcloth again and wipe it away.

Repeat with the other ear.

And that is all you need to do to keep your micro pig clean and happy.

Exercise Needs

Although micro pigs can become lazy, the average micro pig can have a surprising well of energy, usually given in short bursts. Even if your micro pig does not have this, it is still important to take the time to exercise your pig both physically and mentally.

On average, a micro pig should receive about 30 minutes of exercise each day, usually split into two or three smaller sessions of play. Walks are good for pigs, but again, make sure that you have the proper walking permits to take your micro pig off of your property.

In addition to walks, your micro pig should have access to an outdoor yard where he can run and explore on his own. It is important to give him toys to play with since micro pigs are very intelligent and really need to have enrichment toys to keep them from becoming bored.

One of the best things to set up for your micro pig is a sandbox where you bury treasure in. This allows your micro pig to root around in the sand and he will need to find the treats and toys and unearth them from the sand.

Another important toy for a micro pig is a rooting box. This is a wooden box that should be at least 2 feet (0.61 meters) by 2 feet (0.61 meters) in size and should be about 4 inches (10.2 centimetres) in height so your pig can reach it without having to climb in.

Although you can place a number of items in the rooting box, many people find that placing a number of stones into it is the best option, although it is important to make sure that they are not too small to present a choking hazard. Placing food into the rooting box will encourage your pig to root through the box.

In addition to stones, you can place rags, stuffed toys, blankets or towels into the rooting box and give your micro pig a different rooting experience.

Although your pig will love to root, he will need more than simply rooting boxes. Find toys that he can push around and chew on. I find that baby toys designed for children under 18 months are ideal for micro pigs since there is less risk of something small breaking off and posing a choking risk for your pig. While new toys are always wonderful, it is okay to go to a local boot sale or onto eBay to find used toys for your pig to reduce the cost of toys when they are destroyed. Make sure that any used toys you purchase are in good shape and won't pose a choking hazard for your pig.

Lastly, pick up a busy ball for your pig. These are hollow rubber balls that can be filled with treats. As your pig rolls it around, the treats fall out, but only if he rolls it a certain way. The treats will keep him interested and it will stimulate his mind by providing him with a problem to solve.

Chapter Ten: The Healthy Micro Pig

Micro pigs are known to be very healthy animals that have a long lifespan; however, there are a number of health problems that can occur, which a micro pig owner should be aware of.

In this chapter, I will go over some of the more common health problems along with the symptoms and what you need to do if your pig is sick.

The Healthy Pig

A healthy micro pig is always wonderful to see and it is actually very easy to spot a healthy pig amidst a group of other pigs.

The healthy micro pig has bright eyes, is active and has a tail that is looped and not hanging limp. He has a healthy appetite and is constantly on the lookout for a little tidbit or two. A healthy pig is cheerful and his nose is moist. He should have good colouring and should be alert.

Even if your pig is healthy, you should take the time every day to make sure that he stays that way. Purchase a rectal thermometer and check his temperature at the same time every day for about a week. Document it and keep it handy so you can determine your micro pig's average temperature. Once you have those numbers, you can periodically check your pig to make sure that his temperature is still in the healthy range for him.

Do the same visual health check that you did when you purchased your pig. Make sure that he has the appearance of a healthy pig and monitor any signs that he may be sick.

The Sick Pig

Obviously, if your pig is getting sick, you will notice that he isn't as alert or bright as he usually is. His tail may begin to go limp and he may have a dry, cracked nose.

However, besides those signs, there are a few other signs that will let you know something is wrong with your micro pig.

The biggest sign is lack of appetite. If your pig does not want to eat, then you need to monitor him and contact your vet if it continues for more than a day. In fact, it is so unusual for a micro pig not to eat that I would recommend contacting your vet as soon as you notice it. It may be nothing, but then again, it could be a sign of something larger.
Other signs that your pig may be sick are:

- Hunched back so that his hind legs are under his belly when he is standing.
- Unusual behavior.
- High temperature.
- Hair on his back standing on end, even though he is not agitated in any way.

As soon as you see one or more of these signs, seek professional advice immediately.

Common Health Problems with Micro Pigs

Constipation: This is very common with micro pigs, especially during the winter months when your pig is less mobile. A good way to determine if your micro pig has constipation is to break his feces. If it crumbles, then there is a good chance that he is. To treat constipation, give your micro pig more exercise and also offer him some canned pumpkin in his feed. Adding bran to your micro pig's diet will also help with reducing the risk and the symptoms of constipation.

Hypoglycemia: Micro pigs can be prone to hypoglycaemia, which is low glucose or low blood sugar. Symptoms are shaking, irritability, and weakness. It can be treated through diet; however, it is something you will need to monitor throughout your micro pig's life.

Epilepsy: A disease that results in the pig having seizures. Many cases of epilepsy have no known cause and it should be treated from the recommendations of your pig's veterinarian.

Intestinal Blockages: Very common in micro pigs, it is when the food becomes lodged in the intestine and does not move down to the rectum. Symptoms are lethargy, weakness, laying on his side and stretching his legs repeatedly, lack of appetite. This is a very serious condition and requires immediate medical care. The best way to avoid intestinal blockages is to feed your pig small meals. Large meals are usually the cause of an intestinal blockage.

Mites: Another common problem in pet pigs, mites can be very bothersome to a pig and will cause a rash on the skin as well as hair loss. Symptoms are usually a visible rash and your pig will be very itchy and irritable. Mites need to be treated with a medical wash and you will need to treat his bedding and pen as well.

Ticks: All animals can pick up ticks from long grass and pigs are no exception. However, ticks can cause paralysis in pigs and need to be removed as soon as you spot one. Usually, a tick almost looks like a skin tag; however, you can see a small red dot where the tick has burrowed into the skin. Remove by pulling the tick straight out. Do not squeeze the tick or twist it.

Uterine Infections: Not a concern if you have a male, however, females can be susceptible to uterine infections, which is an infection in the uterus. Symptoms are lack of appetite, fatigue, high temperature and many times a discharge from the vulva. It can be life threatening if left untreated and can only be cured with antibiotics. Uterine infections can be avoided if you spay your micro pig.

Cancer: Micro pigs are susceptible to a number of different cancers and they can be difficult to spot, especially if they are not skin cancers. Treatment ranges depending on the type of cancer and should be done by a veterinarian.

Tumors: This is a growth that can either be found on the skin or even inside the pig and includes uterine tumors. Many tumors are benign, however, some can be malignant and it is important to check with your veterinarian if you see a tumor.

Pneumonia: Pigs can be susceptible to illnesses, especially pneumonia and really need a warm and dry place to live. Winter is usually when you see a rise in pneumonia cases so keep your pig in a heated pen during the winter. Many pigs show no signs of pneumonia and usually the first indicator is a lack of appetite. Treatment is through antibiotics.

Salt Poisoning: Finally, salt poisoning is usually in conjunction with drinking water. A pig that eats too much salt will drink too much water and this can lead to fluid in the brain. While you should always have fresh water available to your pig, if you find that he has eaten a lot of salt, give him one cup of water every hour until he is no longer thirsty to slow down the amount of water he drinks.

Spay or Neuter

The final thing that we should look at with your micro pig is whether to spay or neuter your pig. If you are not planning on breeding your pig, then the answer is that you should spay her.

An intact pig can be very hard to manage and a female will go into heat every 3 weeks, or 21 days. This can become very frustrating and will make life with a micro pig harder than it needs to be.

Pigs will mark around and even on people when they are intact and they are at higher risks from some diseases when they are intact.

If you are adopting a male, check to see if the piglet was castrated before he was four weeks old, which is usually less traumatic for the pig. If he hasn't, schedule to have him neutered by the time he is 12 weeks of age. Females should also be spayed around the age of 8 months since it is much more involved and presents a greater risk to your pig.

Remember that you can prevent many of the illnesses through proper care, diet and exercise.

Chapter Eleven: Breeding Your Micro Pig

Although you may have purchased your first micro pig simply because you wanted a pet, after bringing him, or her, home, the thought of breeding may have crossed your mind. If you have, and you feel you could breed pigs, then it is important to really take the time to learn how to properly breed and care for your pig and piglet.

In this chapter, I will go over everything that you will need to know about breeding and raising your own piglets.

Should you breed

Before you begin breeding, you should really decide whether or not this is something that you would like to do. Regardless of your personal views on animal husbandry, breeding has a number of pros and cons and they should be considered before you start breeding.

Pros:

No matter how many cons there are to doing something, there are always a few pros that can make breeding your pig a positive thing. After all, if there were no rewards for breeding, there would be no one breeding pet pigs. However, make sure that all of these pros work for you before you make the final decision to breed your micro pig.

Contributing to a Line: Breeding to add something to an existing line or to preserve a look or temperament that your pig exhibits is often reward enough for breeding. Breeders are often trying to produce a better quality of animal, whether it is looks, temperament or health that they are trying to improve.

Working with Piglets: Let's face it, baby animals are cute and piglets are no exception. Another great pro to breeding is that you get to spend time with baby piglets for the two to three months that they are with you.

Monetary: Although I greatly disagree that there is a monetary gain to breeding piglets, some strains of micro pigs sell for a very large amount of money. Still, you should never expect to make a lot of money on breeding pet pigs.

Sharing Micro Pigs: One of the more rewarding aspects of breeding is being able to share your love of micro pigs with other enthusiasts.

Sustaining your own Line: Lastly, one of the biggest pros to breeding is in sustaining your own line of pigs and ensuring that the pig you love dearly will continue on through her piglets.

Cons:

Like everything, there are a number of cons with breeding and unlike some animals; pigs can have a large number of cons that are unique to them.

Sexually Mature Animals: Although you need your pigs to be sexually mature before you breed them, at times one of the most annoying animals is a sexually mature pig. Males become very aggressive and will try to mount everything. They are constantly trying to get at females and they often lose that wonderful pet pig quality that you had. Females are not usually as aggressive but they can go into heat every few weeks and they become very loud during that time.

Cost: If you take in the number of hours you need to spend with the piglets, the cost of feeding them, caring for the sow, which is the female pig, from a young piglet, vet costs, breeding costs and the countless other expenses that you have breeding pigs, then many times, the amount of money you do make is greatly less than the amount that you spend.

Time: The amount of time that is needed for your litter of piglets can differ from pig to pig but generally, you should expect to spend a lot of time with your piglets to ensure that they are not hurt or become sick.

Work: Raising a litter of piglets can be a lot of work and you can't expect the sow to care for the piglets for the entire time. You will need to change their bedding, some piglets may need to be bottle-fed and others may need more extensive care including medication. You will also need to start socializing them and you will need to find families for the piglets. All of this amounts to a lot of work.

Large Litters: While a large litter may not be a problem, if you can't find homes for them all, then it is definitely a problem for you. Not only will you have to care for a larger litter, which means more time and work, you may find yourself the owner of more pigs than you had ever wanted.

Health Problems: While micro pigs are not known to have difficulty with breeding and birthing piglets, there are still some health risks to breeding and it may add to veterinarian bills. This includes complications during delivery, health problems with your sow and/or health problems with your piglets.

Mess: Although owning any pet is messy, breeding is even messier since you have more than one or two animals to clean up after. Some litters of micro pigs can be quite large and this can lead to even more mess for you to clean up.

Giving up the Piglets: While the goal is to have the piglets adopted, it can be hard to give them up, especially if you, or someone in your family, bonds with one in particular.

Breeding pigs are not for the faint of heart and it takes a large investment both financially and emotionally. It is important to breed because you love micro pigs and feel that you can contribute to the pet population.

You should never breed for monetary reasons or simply to teach your children "the facts of life" since these types of litters often result in the many animals that are put down or sent to shelters every year.

If you are going to breed, do so responsibly from the very beginning.

Good Breeding Practices

Before you start breeding, it is important to pursue proper breeding practices from the start. Although it may seem like this starts right before you begin breeding, it should start before you even bring your piglet home.

Choose your piglet from a reputable breeder who can trace back his pig lines for several generations. Make sure that those lines are very healthy and that there are no known genetic problems in the parents and grandparents.

When you are choosing your breeder, find one who is helpful and let him or her know that you are planning on breeding. Ask for help with the process of breeding your own litter of piglets and in ensuring that your pig is ready for breeding when the time comes.

Once you have your piglet, train and socialize her or him so you have a well rounded pig that people will want to purchase from. Make sure that all of your paperwork is in order and that you have the proper permits to own, breed and have more than one pig on your property at a time.

Before you breed, it is important to have a health check done on both the male and female. Make sure that there are no diseases or health problems that were overlooked on a day to day basis. If there is, do not breed the animals who are sick since illnesses can be transferred to the piglets.

Next, make sure that all of the vaccinations are up to date on your pigs to ensure that they are not susceptible to any diseases while they are carrying a litter. This is particularly important if you are planning on using a male outside of your home.

Lastly, make sure that you have all of the supplies that you will need, including an area for your piglets to be raised, before your sow is even pregnant. Below is a list of supplies that you will need for breeding.

Farrowing Box: Similar in shape and design to a dog whelping box, a farrowing box is used to protect the piglets and provide room for the mamma pig to lie down. It is usually about 5 feet (1.52 meters) wide by 6 feet (1.83 meters) long and is made from 2 x 4 foot board (0.61 by 1.22 meters) on all of the sides. One side of the box will need a low side for your sow to climb into and out of the box easily. On the sides of the box, there should be another 2 x 4 foot board (0.61 by 1.22 meters) box that rests the boards sideways to create a little alcove for the piglets. This provides them with a place to crawl under if they get too hot or if the mama pig is taking up too much room.

Rubber Gloves: When you are delivering a litter, you may need to help the piglet come out of the birth canal. I recommend having a large box of latex gloves for this so you can toss the gloves away after each use.

Iodine: If you have to cut the umbilical cords, then you will need to use iodine to keep the cords clean and to prevent infection.

Baby Vitamin with Iron: All pigs are born with an iron deficiency and they will need to have iron to give them the best start in life.

Towels: For cleaning off the piglets when necessary.

Scissors: A sharp pair of scissors is needed for cutting the umbilical cords. Make sure that they are sterilized before you use them.

KY Jelly: May be necessary for helping the piglet out of the birth canal.

Baby Bottles: Small nipple bottles that have been cleaned and sterilized are important if you have a piglet that is not nursing from the sow.

Goat's Milk: Again, this is good to have on hand in the off chance that you will need to hand feed one of the piglets.

Heat Lamp: A good heat lamp is important to use so the farrowing box is warm and at the ideal temperature to keep your piglets from getting sick.

Scale: Scales are important for keeping track of your piglets. I find that it is important to weigh each piglet shortly after birth and to mark it so you can keep track of their growth.

Ribbon: Depending on the piglets, you may need to secure a piece of different coloured ribbon or yarn around the piglet's neck to keep track of the piglets.

By having everything ready before your pig's birth, you can have the best start for your piglets.

The Breeding Sow

If you have done all your homework, then chances are, you are ready to start breeding. A breeding sow can begin to go into heat by the time she is 5 months of age, although some go into heat much earlier, but you should never breed your pig until she is closer to 2 years for health reasons. Unfortunately, that often means that you could be dealing with an unruly female for a very long time. On a side note, you should never breed a sow after she is 6 to 8 years old for both health and quality of life reasons.

When a sow begins to go into heat, she will usually have a heat every 21 days, or every 3 weeks. A heat usually lasts between 8 to 36 hours so the length of time that you are dealing with a heat is not as long as other animals. In fact, you may not even notice that your sow has come into heat at times.

Signs that your sow is in heat often starts with her becoming unruly. If you have a male pig near a female, she may squeal more and may try to get in with the male. She will be much more restless than she normally is and you may notice that she has a lack of appetite. A physical cue that your sow is in heat is a swollen vulva that is very pink. Lastly, if you press on the sides of her back, she should stand still as though she is accepting a male.

If you choose not to breed her during the heat, there is nothing that you really need to do except keep her away from a male. In a few hours, to a few days, she will be out of heat and she won't come back in for another 21 days, give or take a few.

Before you do breed your sow, make sure that she has proper weight and does not seem thin. If you can see her ribs, and her tail is limp, then there may be signs that she is not at an ideal weight or she is sick. Avoid breeding her until you are sure her health is at the optimal.

Make sure that she has 14 teats. If she has fewer than 14, then you should not breed her since she will require all of them for nursing her piglets.

Another point is to never breed your sow during her very first heat. Allow her to have one or more heats before breeding your sow so that she is an optimal age and at optimal health for breeding.

The longer you wait, the better your sow will be and the healthier your piglets will be.

Once she is in heat, you will need to breed your sow. Some may need to be artificially inseminated, while others will need special intervention.

You will always need to have the proper travelling documents if you are breeding your pig to a male off of your site. The general rule of thumb is that the female should be taken to the male. Boars, a male pig used for breeding, don't usually perform their breeding duties in a place they are not familiar with.

If you have the boar for breeding, you may need to create a breeding crate for the sow and boar so that they cannot move away from each other or turn away. This will enable the breeding to go easier for both you and the sow.

Occasionally, even with a sow that is in a full heat, a boar will not perform his duty. This is usually when veterinarian care is necessary to ensure that your sow does become pregnant. There are two ways that this can be accomplished including hormones or drugs that will help the boar become interested in breeding or artificial insemination where semen is collected and inserted into the sow through the use of a medical device.

Some breeding may only be done through artificial insemination with the semen being sent to your veterinarian for use with your sow. Many breeders are opting for artificial insemination since this limits the number of diseases their sows are exposed to and enables them to choose the best boar from anywhere in the world.

Finally, a boar and sow can simply be placed together several times during the heat and allowed to mate naturally without any intervention, although this may not always work as planned.

Regardless of how you are breeding your sow, make sure that both animals are in optimal health and that they are exceptional examples of your pig breed.

Caring for the Pregnant Sow

Now that you have bred your sow, you are probably wondering if she is pregnant. Unfortunately, it can be very difficult to tell if she is pregnant or not until she is several weeks along in her pregnancy. The best rule of thumb is to assume that she is pregnant and care for her like she is during that time.

Generally, the first indication that your sow is pregnant is a lack of heat. After 21 days, if your sow does not go into heat, then she is pregnant.

During this time, care does not change significantly and your pig can go about her day as she normally would. Although pigs do have a shorter gestation time, which is a term used to describe the length of pregnancy, than many animals, they are much longer than dogs and cats.

In fact, gestation for a pig is usually between 110 to 115 days on average. During the first few weeks, diet and care remain the same, however, during the final few weeks, some changes need to be made.

The biggest change is your sow's access to grass and soil. While you may have a designated section in your garden for your sow, it is important to offer her fresh grass and new soil several times per week. This is important so she gets the right amount of nutrients every day for her and her growing litter of piglets.

When she is closer along in her pregnancy, your sow's teats will begin to enlarge and they may even begin dragging on the ground. This is a good indication that you should make some changes to your environment if you haven't already.

While the teats will toughen up as they rub on the ground, you will want to prevent your sow from climbing up on things where her teats may be cut. Installing a ramp near your stairs is better than her having to climb up the stairs pregnant.

You may need to wash the teats closer to the delivery date since a milk line will begin to form on the teats and the moisture may pick up excess dirt and debris while she is walking.

Make sure that you keep her confined to her farrowing area during the last week before delivery and only let her out for her exercise when you are with her. She should still receive about 30 minutes of exercise each day but it should be in a controlled manner.

Lastly, her bedding will need to be refreshed on a daily basis the closer she gets to her farrowing (birthing) date.

Feeding

Like the daily care, feeding your pregnant sow is not very different than feeding your breeding sow. Make sure that she gets plenty of greens and usually you can increase her greens intake by about 5%.

You do not need to use a pig food for pregnant sows, however, they are formulated better and are something that I would recommend. Regardless of the feed you are using, you should feed your pregnant sow about 3% of her body weight in cups. Make sure that you only increase the amount of food once you know that she is pregnant.

In addition to her regular food, you may need to give her one chewable children's multivitamin to ensure that all of her vitamin and mineral needs are met through the pregnancy.

A few days before your sow is expected to deliver, start reducing her feed slightly and add bran to her diet to work as a laxative. Usually a ¼ of the cup of bran and a ¼ of a cup less food is enough of a reduction.

Lastly, fresh clean drinking water is a must for your sow at all times in her life but especially when she is pregnant.

Farrowing

Although you do have a fair amount of time to wait for your piglets to be born, it is important to get ready for their arrival a few weeks before your sow's actual due date.

To start, make sure that her farrowing area is clean and free of any pests. Start by cleaning the entire room with a solution of 2 % of phenyl lotion and water. Also scrub down the farrowing box.

Once it is clean, spray it down again to make sure that you have caught any pests that were missed the first time through. It is important that you keep the farrowing box vacant for about a week after cleaning so I recommend that you clean it and prepare it 2 to 3 weeks before your sow is due.

After the box is clean, it is time to get your sow ready. Start by deworming her about 3 weeks before farrowing. Do not allow her into the farrowing box until she has been dewormed to prevent the worms from affecting your piglets.

About ten days before your sow is due, wash her down and clean her completely to make sure that there is no dirt or parasites on her. Once she is dry, you can move her into the farrowing room and an outside farrowing pen. Do not allow her into her normal pen, especially if she shares that area with another pig.

A few days before the farrowing, get your supplies together and wash them. Make sure that you sterilize them in hot water and wrap them to keep them clean. You can set up a heat lamp in the farrowing box but make sure that it can't be hit or knocked into the box. A heat lamp is a must for keeping your piglets warm and preventing illnesses in them.

2 to 3 days before your sow is due, chop straw up and place it in the farrowing box. Make sure that you keep it clean and that you do not use too much of it come the time that your piglets are due. They can easily become lost in the hay and may be crushed by the mama sow because of this.

During the days leading up to your sow's delivery date, keep a close eye on her. I recommend that you keep a close eye on her for the week leading up to her delivery so you can be close at hand when she does go into labour.

Signs that your sow is going into labour are:

- *Restlessness:* She will begin to pace and seem very unlike herself when she is ready to give birth.

- *Nesting:* During the days leading up to her delivery, your sow will begin to nest and try to make her farrowing box comfortable for herself. Make sure that she is in the farrowing box and not trying to get into a different place to deliver her piglets.

When it is time for your sow to deliver, make sure that you sit back during the delivery. Many sows are quite efficient and having an owner close by can actually make them nervous, causing delays and problems during the delivery.

The best thing to do is sit to the side where you won't be bothering your sow but close enough where you can see into the farrowing box easily. Soothe your sow with your voice but don't get too involved unless necessary. Many sows will bite in an effort to protect her piglets.

Labor usually lasts 24 hours, although some are shorter, and there are set stages during farrowing that you need to be aware of.

Stage One: Pre-farrowing

This usually begins 10 to 14 days before your sow begins to farrow. This is when you see many of the signs that I have already mentioned including the restlessness and the growth of her mammary glands.

The pre-farrowing period continues until your sow is ready to deliver her piglets.

Usually, the pre-farrowing stage will produce a mucous discharge from the vulva and this is a sign that parturition, when the piglets have begun to move into the birth canal, has begun. On a side note, if you spot any feces in the mucus, it is a strong indicator that the first piglet will be born backwards. If this is the case, it is imperative that you contact your vet and have her checked.

Stage Two: Farrowing

This is the active labor and is when the piglets are being delivered. During this stage, a piglet will usually be born every 10 to 20 minutes and usually lasts between 3 to 8 hours, although it can last longer.

During the farrowing process, it is important to watch your sow very closely and to make sure that there is nothing complicating her delivery. Generally, there is a longer gap between the first and second piglet, however, if the gap is over an hour, it is important to contact your veterinarian to find out if she will need medical intervention or not.

While you may not need to be involved, be prepared to do so and you should be ready to care for the piglets as soon as they are born. Usually, sows are not very attentive to piglets as they are birthing and they may overlook or crush a piglet as they are delivering the next one.

The process for farrowing is as follows.

1. The sow begins to labor and is restless.

2. The sow lies on her side to prepare for the birth of a piglet. She may simply lie down but usually a sow will begin to shiver and will lift her back leg as she labors.

3. The sow will begin to twitch her tail and will push the piglet out, minus the afterbirth.

4. Immediately after the piglet is born, it is important to pick it up and towel it dry since the sow will not do this.

5. Take the iodine and dip the umbilical cord into it to prevent infections for the piglet.

6. Do a quick health check on the piglet, making sure that you get the piglets weight and that you check to make sure that the piglet is not in distress in any way.

7. Place a drop of the baby vitamin with iron, about 1 ml of it, into the piglet's mouth and make sure that the piglet swallows it.

8. Place the piglet into a box that is under a heat lamp to keep him warm. Usually, a piglet will be ready to nurse within a half hour of being born so keep an eye on them and place them back on the mother when they are ready to nurse, unless she is delivering a piglet at that time. For piglets that appear too weak to nurse, try bottle feeding.

9. While you are working with the piglet, your sow will be recovering from the delivery and getting ready for the next one. Every sow is different and she may move around, rest or become very restless. As she is recovering, offer her soothing words and clean up the farrowing box. Many sows will go to the bathroom in the farrowing box during delivery so you will need to clean up the mess and put in clean straw if it becomes too soiled.

10. Never place the piglets into the box as the sow is delivering the next piglet.

Generally, a sow will deliver 8 to 13 piglets, although some can have more and some can have less. It is important to realize that pigs have a very high mortality rate and it is estimated that 25% of the piglets will be stillborn or will die within the first few days of delivery. Be prepared for this when your sow is delivering.

Stage Three: End of Farrowing

At this stage of the farrowing, all of the piglets will be delivered and the sow will begin delivering all of the placenta. Pigs are not like some other animals who deliver a baby and the placenta each time and instead, they usually deliver all of the piglets before they deliver all of the placentas.

The placentas are delivered over a time period of 1 to 4 hours and you will need to remove it from the farrowing box as she delivers it. One thing to note is that some of the afterbirth will be delivered with a piglet so if you find that there doesn't seem to be a lot of afterbirth during this stage; she probably passed it with the piglets.

Once the afterbirth is delivered, your sow will begin to get into the routine of being a mother. She will still have a heavy, bloody discharge for a few days after the delivery, usually between 3 to 5 days, but she will be eating normally and will be behaving in her regular manner.

After she has finished farrowing, she will usually lay on her side and start grunting and calling the piglets. This is when you will be able to place the piglets back into the farrowing box with her. If she is still shivering and moving her hind leg, then she is still farrowing.

After the delivery, it is important to keep track of your piglets and your sow to ensure that everything is okay. If she seems to be losing weight or is bleeding heavily, then she may have a complication and will need to see immediate veterinarian care.

If not, then simply keep an eye on her and make sure her and the piglets are comfortable by keeping the farrowing box at a cozy 80 to 90°F temperature.

Complications during Farrowing

Like any type of breeding program, breeding micro pigs is not free of complications. There are a number that can occur that can mean life or death for your sow or your piglets.

It is important to be aware of the complications, the signs of the complications and how to deal with so you can ensure that your sow has the least risk involved with delivering her piglets. Please note that many complications must be treated by someone experienced with pigs or by a veterinarian. If you do not have the experience, make sure that you have a vet on standby when your sow is delivering her piglets.

Some of the more common complications with farrowing are:

Rotation of Horns: The uterus of a sow consists of two horns, which are part of the uterus where the uterine tubes connect and it is where the piglets are developed. One problem that can occur is that the one horn will cross over the other and will create a pouch of piglets that cannot be moved into the birth canal on their own. The signs that this has happened is with the sow pushing and straining but being unable to pass a piglet through for over a half hour to an hour.

The only way to determine if it is the case is by placing your hand into the cervix while your sow is standing and feeling for the pouch of piglets that is formed. If you feel one, the piglets need to be moved up out of the horn with your hand and then allow your sow to deliver a piglet. If she still does not deliver a piglet, then you may have to repeat the process or decide on another medical intervention. I only recommend that you work the piglets if you know what you are doing. If you don't, consult your vet.

Uterine Inertia: This is when contractions have stopped, even though there are piglets that still need to be delivered. Generally, uterine inertia is caused when there is more than one piglet in the cervix waiting to be born. The only way to correct it is by helping the piglets out. To do this, simply place your hand over the head of the piglet, placing your first and second fingers around the neck and then pulling down out of the cervix. If the piglet is rear presented, then place your fingers around the hock and pull down. You may only need to help the one piglet out to get the contractions started again; however, you may also need to remove all of the piglets that are crammed into the cervix.

Too Large: At times, a piglet may be too large to pass easily through the cervix and will need to be helped out. If this happens, the best method is to take a clean and disinfected nylon cord and loop it at one end. Place it in the cervix and bring it over the ears of the piglet and then down under the piglet's jaw. Carefully pull the cord down to help the piglet out. You may need to lubricate the piglet with KY Jelly to make it easier for the piglet to be removed.

Failure to Breathe: If the piglet is born and it is not breathing, you may have to stimulate the breathing. There are two ways to do this and it depends on what is going on. First, insert a piece of straw into the nose and poke it up slightly. This should make the piglet cough and will remove anything that is blocking the windpipe. If this does not work, place your hand around the piglet's head and put your finger in his mouth to hold his tongue forward. Hold the piglet by his back legs with your other hand and swing him. This will force any mucus out of his throat so he is able to breathe.

If you find at any time that you had to do an internal examination or manipulation during the farrowing, you should administer an antibiotic injection to your sow at the end of the delivery to stave off any infection that may occur.

Even after giving the injection, keep an eye on your sow over the next 24 hours to ensure that an infection does not set in.

The Piglets

Now that you have made it through the farrowing process, it is time to start caring for your piglets. If you were lucky, you could have a good sized litter to care for and although the mother takes over most of your piglet's care, you will still need to do your share of work.

Again, it is important to remember that pigs do have a high mortality rate. Piglets are susceptible to illness and they are commonly crushed by the mother pig when she shifts around in the nest. Some piglets are weaker than others and may need to be hand fed to ensure that they are getting enough milk to thrive.

When we look at caring for your piglets, it is better to break it up into stages since your piglets will be going through 6 to 8 weeks of developmental stages from birth to weaning.

Stage One: Newborn

During the first few hours and days of your piglet's life, there are a few things that you should keep track of. First is how your mama pig is doing. Is she feeding the piglets? Does she seem attentive to them? Are all the piglets getting equal shares? If they are

not, begin taking the piglet out of the box for bottle feeding of goat's milk several times a day. Some piglets may need to be bottle fed completely and this will mean that you need to feed your piglets every two hours.

If you have multiple sows delivering piglets around the same time, it is a good idea to transfer the piglets around between the litters. Sows with small litters can take some of the piglets from the larger litters to ensure that all the piglets have the best chance. It is very important that if you do transfer your piglets that you only transfer the largest piglets to ensure that the smaller ones have a better chance at life.

When you do transfer, make sure that it is only across litters that are farrowing within the same week, never more than one or two days apart so the piglets receive the colostrum that they need.

The first week is the time when you will be doing much of the upkeep and it really depends on what you prefer for your pigs.

Within the first few days, take the time to clip the needle teeth that piglets have. These are very sharp and can injure the sow's teats. Be careful not to crush the tooth but simply clip off the lips of the teeth to keep them dull.

During the first day, if you are docking the tail, now is the time to do it. Many vets will do the tail simply by cutting the tail with side-cutter pliers until it is ¼ inch (0.6 centimeters) long.

During the first week, take the weight of the piglets to ensure that they are growing steadily. If any seem like they are lacking in weight, simply supplement their nursing with bottle feeding as well.

Since piglets are born with an iron deficiency, give the piglets one millilitre of baby vitamin every day for the first week to ensure that they are getting the nutrients for healthy growth.

Stage Two: First Few Weeks

During the first few weeks, there is not a lot that you have to do. Make sure you check the piglets daily to ensure proper growth and to catch any potential problems early.

By the time your piglets are 2 weeks of age, you can start introducing creep feed to their diets. This is a specially formulated feed that is offered to piglets along with water as an additional food for them. It is called creep feeding simply because it is placed in an area where the piglets can reach it but the sow cannot.

It should be given according to the recommendations by your vet and also according to the recommendations on the packaging. Some breeders prefer to make their own creep feed by starting with goat's milk and baby cereal in a pan. The first few days of creep feeding is a very diluted combination, more milk than cereal, and then it is combined until the piglets are weaned.

During the first few weeks, make sure that you spend time with the piglets, handling them and getting them socialized to new things. The better socialized they are, the better the chance of them becoming well rounded pets.

It is also important to keep the room clean and dry. Sows are not known for cleaning up the nesting box and it is up to you to remove any dirt, debris and feces from the box. You will need to keep the room at a steady 80 to 90°F temperature since young piglets cannot generate their own heat.

Stage Three: Weaning

Although weaning usually starts in the first few weeks of piglet's lives when you introduce creep feed, a piglet should be fully weaned by the time he is 6 to 8 weeks.

It is important that you do not send the piglet to a new home until he is fully weaned at around 8 weeks of age. If you do, there can be serious risks for the piglet and the new owners may end up having to pay large sums of money in vet bills.

Since you have already introduced creep into your piglet's diets, weaning is actually a very easy stage to work through.

Start by giving your piglets creep and then start giving them pig pellets. I find the best way to do this is to grind the pellets into a powder and make a mushy cereal with goat's milk and the pellets. Place it on a spoon and feed it to the pigs or in a pan.

Strangely, many piglets prefer to eat from a white pan than a colored or black pan so make sure that you choose one that works for your piglets. You may have to push your piglet's snout down into the food to get them started but they will quickly learn how to eat it.

After a few days, begin to add moist, whole pig pellets into the food. Give them more feedings in the day and reduce access to the sow to prevent them from nursing too much.

Continue on this way until they are eating pellets and are not nursing from your sow. Make sure that you provide your piglets with plenty of fresh water throughout the day to ensure that they do not get dehydrated.

During the weaning stage, you should be spending time with the piglets and getting them conditioned to a range of noises, people and experiences. Remember that they are still susceptible to health problems and need to be kept in a warm and dry place until they are 8 weeks of age and ready to go to their new home.

If you are offering the service to your potential piglet owners, now is a good time to castrate any of the male piglets that you have. In fact, it is less traumatic for a piglet to be castrated before he is 4 weeks of age.

If you aren't, make sure that you let all potential owners know that they haven't been castrated.

In the end, there is nothing more rewarding than raising your own piglets and finding them a new home. It can be a wonderful experience and while there is a lot of work and many highs and lows to raising a litter of piglets, you will find it was well worth it.

Chapter Twelve: The Senior Micro Pig

When you first bring home your micro pig, you are probably only thinking about the cute and sweet little piglet that is capturing your heart. Sure, you are probably thinking about the training and all of the other tasks that you will need to do as a new pig owner, however, you may not be thinking about a senior pig.

In fact, the thoughts of a senior pig may be a long ways off since many micro pigs can live a long and healthy life up until they are close to 18 or more years old.

Despite the fact that caring for an aging pig is still in the distant future, it is important to be prepared to do so.

Before you purchase your piglet, remind yourself that this is a lifelong commitment. Your piglet will be with you for nearly two decades and the later stages of life will need more care and dedication than the earlier stages, even when he is a piglet.

I am not saying this to scare you, by any means, but it is an important fact that should be emphasised. Pigs grow old and while their care is similar to what it has always been, there are a few considerations that you should make for them.

Feeding your Aging Pig

Feeding your micro pig may change slightly as your pig begins to age and it really depends on your pig. If you find that he is as active as he always was, then you can still feed him as you would always feed him. However, if he is starting to slow down and is becoming obese because of it, you will need to reduce the amount of food he gets in a day.

Generally, a micro pig should eat about 2% of his body weight when he is becoming overweight. This means that he will be eating less than ½ a cup of food every day.

A senior pig's teeth are not always as strong as they used to be and it is better to give him food and snacks that are easier to chew and swallow. Soft vegetables and fruit are good treats, as are raisins. Make sure that you give your micro pig extra bran and that he gets plenty of access to fresh water.

Another good idea is to give your micro pig a chewable children's vitamin every day to ensure that he is getting all of the nutrients and vitamins that he needs.

Setting up the Environment for Your Aging Pig

When your pig begins to grow old, he is going to have a little more difficulty navigating the world around him than he did when he was younger. During this time, you are going to have to look at ways to make the world much more comfortable for him.

One of the biggest hurdles that a senior pig will have are stairs. As they grow older, stairs will become more difficult for your micro pig to climb and you should consider putting in a ramp for him so he can get into and out of his pen easily.

Your senior pig will need a warmer place to sleep. Make sure that it is at a good temperature of about 80°F and that it is dry and out of the wind. A senior pig is much more susceptible to illnesses and will need to be kept away from younger pigs who may have been exposed.

Make sure that your senior micro pig has plenty of fresh and clean grass and soil to root through and graze on. The higher quality the soil is, the less likely he will be at risk for selenium and many other vitamins and minerals. If you need to, shift his pig pen slightly in your garden so he has access to new grass while the old grass recovers from his grazing.

Lastly, your senior pig still needs exercise to keep him healthy but it should be in moderation and should be light exercise so it doesn't stress his joints.

Short walks two or three times a day is ample exercise for a pig but don't be afraid to offer your pig a few toys or to get him playing in the backyard. Yes, the exercise will be lighter and will only be 5 to 10 minute intervals but playing with your senior pig will keep him young.

Owning a micro pig is a rewarding experience and one that you will cherish throughout your pig's life. There is no other pet that combines a cute snout, cheerful little squeals and a curly little tail with the loyalty and intelligence that is found in a micro pig.

Chapter Thirteen: Common Pig Terms

So you are interested in owning a pig, well if you want to be a true pig lover and owner, it is important to understand a few of the common pig terms that you will hear the moment you enter the pig raising world. Below is a list of terms and words that you will experience in the pig world.

Afterbirth: The tissue that is delivered after the birth of a sow's piglets. It includes the placenta and fetal membranes.

Anemia: A disease caused by the lack of iron in the blood, very common in piglets.

Barrow: A castrated male pig.

Blowing Coat: A term used to describe shedding of the pig's hair or coat.

Boar: An intact (uncastrated) male pig

Castration: Removing a male pig's testicles

Colostrum: A milk that is high in antibodies which is produced during the first few days after the piglets are born.

Creep Feeding: A feed that is placed in an area where the piglets can reach it but the sow cannot.

Crossbreeding: Mating of two distinct breeds of pigs.

Dewclaw: The small hooves that are found on the back of the foot, usually there are two hooves.

Estrus: Part of the reproductive cycle, this is when the female is most receptive to males.

Farrow: Term used to describe a sow giving birth.

Farrowing Box: A designed box where the sow gives birth to her piglets.

Gestation: The period of time that pregnancy takes, usually between 110 to 115 days.

Inbreeding: Mating closely related pigs.

Lactation: When milk is produced in a sow that is nursing or about to give birth.

Line Breeding: Breeding two pigs that are related through the same family line but are not as closely related as pigs who are used for inbreeding.

Mohawk: The hair on the midline of the pig that rises when the pig is agitated.

Monogastric: A simply stomach digestive system.

Needle Teeth: Tiny, sharp teeth that are present at birth. Piglets are usually born with eight and all eight teeth need to be trimmed to prevent injury to the sow's teats.

Overlaying: When a sow crushes her young by laying on them.

Ovulation: When the ova are released during the estrus period of reproductive cycle.

Piglets: Baby pig.

Rooting: A natural behaviour where the pig pushes his snout into the ground to pull things up.

Shoat: Young pig.

Sow: An adult female pig, usually refers to one that has given birth.

Stag: A boar after he has been castrated as an adult.

Standing Heat: A stage of estrus when the sow will allow a male to mount her.

Tusk: Canine teeth of a pig that are found on both the upper and lower jaws. Generally, they curve and grow upwards.

Vulva: Female genitalia

Wallow: A place for a pig to lie in to cool off. Usually it is a mud hole.

Photo Credits:

Cover: © Michaela Stejskalova | Dreamstime.com
Page 9 and 44: © Oksana Tumeniuk | Dreamstime.com
Page 15: © Martina Berg | Dreamstime.com
Page 16: © Phant | Dreamstime.com
Page 19 and 121: © Aleksas Kvedoras | Dreamstime.com
Page 23: © Eric Isselée | Dreamstime.com
Page 28: © Eriklam | Dreamstime.com, © Eric Isselée | Dreamstime.com
Page 31: © Joseph Salonis | Dreamstime.com
Page 35: © Catalin Plesa | Dreamstime.com
Page 40: © Musat Christian | Dreamstime.com
Page 41: © T.h. Klimmeck | Dreamstime.com
Page 46 and 133: © Jablko1 | Dreamstime.com
Page 52: © Richard Thomas | Dreamstime.com
Page 55: © Vasyl Helevachuk | Dreamstime.com
Page 58 and 108: © Grygoriev Vitalii | Dreamstime.com
Page 63: © Gynane | Dreamstime.com
Page 68 and 167: © Studio 37 | Dreamstime.com
Page 71: © Matt Antonino | Dreamstime.com
Page 76: © Renata Osińska | Dreamstime.com
Page 79: © Eric Isselée | Dreamstime.com
Page 84: © Mircea Bezergheanu | Dreamstime.com
Page 91: © Bigpressphoto | Dreamstime.com
Page 99: © Vasyl Helevachuk | Dreamstime.com
Page 100: © Vasyl Helevachuk | Dreamstime.com
Page 104: © Elena Koulik | Dreamstime.com

CPSIA information can be obtained at www.ICGtesting.com
Printed in the USA
BVOW09s1036201214

380037BV00004B/39/P